RIDING FOR JUSTICE

The mining town of King Creek sits in the heart of the Nevada gold-fields. It has no law to speak of but Stover's Law — ruthlessly enforced by one greedy woman, her three callous sons, and a dozen hired gunmen. The Stover family is systematically fleecing the townsfolk of everything they have, with anyone standing in their way either bought off — or killed off. In desperation, Pearl Denton turns to her old friend, legendary town-tamer Sam Judge, for help . . .

BEN BRIDGES

RIDING FOR JUSTICE

Complete and Unabridged

LINFORD
Leicester

First published in Great Britain in 1990
This revised edition published in 2016

First Linford Edition
published 2017

A catalogue record for this book is available
from the British Library.

ISBN 978–1–4448–3448–2

Published by
F. A. Thorpe (Publishing)
Anstey, Leicestershire

Set by Words & Graphics Ltd.
Anstey, Leicestershire
Printed and bound in Great Britain by
T. J. International Ltd., Padstow, Cornwall

This book is printed on acid-free paper

1

The door to Stover's General Store crashed open and a skinny little miner came sailing out into the street.

He was maybe forty years old, and dressed in a worn broadcloth jacket and patched gray pants. He flew off the low boardwalk and hit the churned-up mud of Main Street in a clumsy, painful belly-flop.

His yelp ended in a gurgle.

The breath left him in a rush.

For a moment he saw only stars. Then, with a struggle, he managed to sit up and turn himself around. It wasn't going to be so easy to regain his feet, though, so for the time being he would have to continue his argument from a sitting position.

'*Stover!*' he yelled. Blood dribbled down his chin from a split lip, and a bruise smudged his left cheek, just visible beneath the sparse, dust-colored whiskers that shaded his narrow jaw. 'Come on out here, you sonofabitch!'

The street — little more than a meager, winding gap between two rows of mismatched wood or canvas dwellings — was busy. High-sided wagons rumbled and slid slowly through the mud. The miner, brushing a few thin strands of hair back from his forehead, had to shout to make himself heard above all the bustle, and the steady pounding of stamp-mills at work on the ridges to the west.

'*Stover! You hear me?*'

Townsfolk — mostly men, but a few hard-faced women as well — barely paused to watch the ruckus. Most had seen enough similar trouble in the last couple of months, and were in no hurry to witness more.

There was maybe a gap of five or six heartbeats. Then the miner heard footsteps coming from inside the store. Again he struggled to rise to his feet, the look on his thin, ruddy face suggesting that maybe he'd started doubting the wisdom of having called Stover outside.

At last a figure appeared in the doorway, tall, stocky, with short brown hair slicked down on a round head and a white apron tied across his fancy red vest. If the sign above the door was anything to go by, this was most likely Randolph P. Stover, the proprietor of the store. But his flinty brown eyes, his hard, high cheekbones and the surly lips beneath his thick handlebar moustache made him look more like a road agent.

'You still here, Harrigan?' he asked mildly. He was in his mid-thirties, something of a dandy judging by the diamond stick-pin in his sky-blue cravat. Two men followed him out onto the boardwalk, younger, leaner, troublemakers for sure. They flanked Stover like obedient bird-dogs, hooking thumbs in their pistol-belts and grinning down at the figure in the mud.

The miner, Harrigan, finally stumbled up onto his feet, rediscovering some of his earlier fury. 'Damn right I'm still here!' he snapped defiantly. 'And for the last time, I'll thank you to take my custom — and charge me a fair price!'

Stover's moustache shifted slightly as his surly lips reshaped themselves into a disdainful smile. 'My prices *are* fair,' he said quietly.

'The hell you say!' Harrigan retorted. 'You're charging well over the odds for your stock, Stover, and you know it!'

'Then buy your supplies someplace else.'

Harrigan's angry blue eyes dropped away from the storekeeper's face. 'There *is* noplace else,' he hissed through clenched teeth. 'That's the trouble.'

Stover's smile turned into a smirk. 'Well, then,' he said. 'You want supplies, Harrigan, you pay the asking price. Understand? You pay up and you keep quiet. You don't go insulting honest merchants, or making accusations you can't back up. And one other thing — you pay in cash or dust. I don't allow credit.'

Harrigan shook his head in disbelief and took a couple of shaky paces back to the boardwalk. 'There ought to be a law against people like you,' he persisted, virtually repeating what he'd already said inside. 'You're vultures. Profiteers. You get a town sewn up good and tight, then you bleed every mother's son in it dry!'

Stover shrugged and said unconcernedly, 'It's one way to make a living, isn't it?'

He turned his back on Harrigan and took a pace back into the store before the miner reached out and clapped a mud-caked palm on his shoulder. 'Don't turn your back on me, damn you!' he rasped. 'I haven't finished with you yet — !'

Stover wheeled around to confront the miner eyeball-on. His lips compressed and his brown eyes fairly glittered. 'Take your filthy paws off me!' he spat, brushing at the damp brown stain on his once-white sleeve. 'Baker, Coltrain — get this pest off my premises!'

Stover's bully-boys needed no second urging. Baker, the shorter of the two, who wore a well-used Merwin & Hulbert Army .44 high on his left hip, shoved Harrigan away from the storekeeper. Coltrain, tall, tanned and, like his partner, somewhere in his mid-twenties, followed up with a swift right jab to the miner's belly.

Harrigan grunted and folded forward, clutching at his punished stomach. His eyes screwed shut and his mouth stretched taut over his yellowed teeth. While he was frozen in that position, Baker sent a knuckly fist into the miner's face, and Harrigan went over backwards, landing in the mud for the second time in five minutes.

Harrigan's mind was in a whirl. One moment he saw Stover smirking at him;

the next he saw the blue Nevada sky, dotted with breeze-driven clouds. A second later he was flat on his back, gasping, trying to roll away from the hooves of two trotting horses, into whose path he had fallen.

'*Whoa, there!*'

It must have been Harrigan's lucky day, because the riders somehow managed to rein in before their horses snapped him like kindling. But his relief was short-lived, for no sooner had the horses drawn to a halt than Coltrain was down beside him, and putting a boot to his ribs.

As Harrigan curled into a ball, the newcomers took in the scene from beneath their hat-brims. Three kicks later, the younger of the two decided he'd seen enough.

'Hey, you there! Any more of that an' you'll kill him!'

Coltrain paused with his left foot drawn back for another wallop. He had a long, sharp-featured face and icy blue eyes in which the pupils seemed to be the single most prominent feature. The hair spilling from beneath his smoke-gray J.B. was the color of straw, as was the light stubble etching his pointed jaw. He wore a gray shirt, old denim pants, low-heeled boots, a black leather rig holding a Colt's .45 tied tight to his right thigh.

For a moment he just stared up at the rider; he saw a kid maybe two years his junior, nothing more. Then he said, 'You talkin' to *me*?'

The youngster up on the sturdy little cow-pony nodded very slowly. 'Reckon so,' he allowed.

On the boardwalk, Stover eyed the newcomers more carefully. Coltrain might only see an old man and a boy. Stover saw more. He saw the twin Tranters in the kid's knotted-down *buscadero* holsters, the smooth grips of the older man's Remington .44, and something inside him tingled in warning. These two weren't just another pair of miners hoping to try their luck in the gold-fields around King Creek; they

8

were something *more*.

He took a slow step forward, allowing his flinty brown eyes to travel from one trail-worn face to the other. 'I appreciate your concern,' he said diplomatically. 'But this here's none of your business. It's a private matter; understand me?'

The young rider nodded once more. Like his companion, he had a long, slightly mournful face, but while it was certainly lived in, it was also painfully innocent as well. His chin was strong and square, pitted by a dimple, and his build seemed compact and whippy. 'Sure,' he said. 'I don't dispute that for a minute. But whether you're settlin' a private matter or not, you're goin' about it in an awful public way. Besides which, I'd say that feller down there's taken enough.' His stormcloud-gray eyes flicked back to settle on Coltrain. 'Was I you,' he said pointedly, 'I'd stand back an' give him some air.'

'The hell you — '

'I mean it, partner,' the young man warned.

Coltrain's wolfish face set itself into a smile. 'I'd like to see you try an' stop me,' he growled. And once again he raised his left foot in preparation for another kick.

The young man up on the cow-pony knew a challenge when he heard one. But what he chose to do about it was so unexpected that Coltrain never even saw it coming.

Gigging his horse a foot or so closer, he slipped his own left boot free of the stirrup and kicked Coltrain right in the face. The blue-eyed bully-boy grunted, fell backwards, hit his head on the edge of the boardwalk and almost lost consciousness.

'Well?' The young man on the cow-pony asked mildly. 'How do *you* like it?'

Coltrain spat blood. 'Why, you — '

With his temper up, he made a move towards his Colt. On the boardwalk beside Stover, Baker did likewise.

Before either of them could clear leather, however, the kid's older companion had his Remington out and covering them.

'I wouldn't,' he advised quietly.

They didn't.

For one split second the shock was plain on their faces, even Harrigan's. None of them had seen the older man draw. If they hadn't known such a thing to be impossible, they might have sworn that the .44 had just leapt up into his palm.

'Now,' said the oldster calmly. 'Reach across and unlimber those guns. Slowly, now, and with your fingertips only! That's better. Now toss 'em down here in the street.'

Baker glanced at the thick, wrinkly mud and a look of anger tightened his hard face. 'You — '

'Do it,' the oldster recommended softly.

'I'll be damned first!' hissed Baker.

The fellow up on the roan sighed and thumbed back the Remington's hammer. 'All right,' he said equably. 'If that's the way you want it.'

His eyes grew bleak and dangerous.

The air around Stover's store grew electric. Then the moment passed and Baker and Coltrain reluctantly tossed their sidearms into the street.

The older man nodded his satisfaction. He looked to be just a little taller than his partner, six feet two, maybe more, and he was raw-boned, hard-muscled, perhaps forty-five years of age. He had a lean, weatherbeaten face and surprisingly gentle gray eyes. His accent was Texan, his dress that of a range-rider. But his manner was authoritative, and he handled trouble like a man who'd had much practice.

Who was he, then, Stover wondered. A lawman of some kind?

'That's better,' the fellow said, breaking in on the storekeeper's thoughts. He peered over the head of his roan and addressed Harrigan. 'You all right down there, pilgrim?'

Harrigan got awkwardly to his feet,

holding his ribs. 'Sure . . . sure . . . much obliged to you — '

'Forget it. Just get the hell out of here.'

Harrigan bobbed his head. But before he picked up his fallen hat and made tracks, he pointed a trembly finger at Stover. 'Just you remember,' he said in a low voice. 'I ain't finished with you yet, Stover. You'll pay for roughin' me up, just like you'll pay for gyppin' decent folks. I swear it!'

And so saying, he turned on his heel and struggled off through the mud.

'Now,' the older of the two riders said into the silence. 'Guess we'll be movin' along, too. But let's just get one thing straight. Far as we're concerned, this little wrangle ends *here*. You got that?'

Stover nodded grimly.

'Just so's you know,' the oldster muttered, reholstering his sidearm. He touched the brim of his round-crowned, buff-colored Stetson politely. 'Good-day to you, then.'

Coltrain snorted. 'Go to hell!'

And Sam Judge, the man Ned Buntline himself had once hailed as 'The Prince of the Pistoleers', paused to offer him a mirthless smile. 'If all I hear about King Creek is true,' he replied gravely, 'I'd say that's just about where we *have* ended up.'

* * *

By anyone's estimate, King Creek was a shambles.

For a start, most of the commercial businesses were still operating from out of mud-splattered tents. Here was a laundry run by some chattering Chinese; there stood three, no, *four* independent assay offices and about a dozen makeshift eateries. Further along the street some enterprising soul had erected a whole block of frame dwellings, many still in the process of completion. There were three hostelries, eight or nine saloons, two bawdyhouses and a tent housing the crude but tidy office of the *King Creek*

Clarion. Glancing around, Sam and his youthful companion, Matt Dury, saw more shingles than they could shake a stick at, advertising everything from attorneys and spiritualists to liquor dealers selling real St Louis Lager.

But then, gold lured scavengers just as much as it lured the men who craved to mine it, and Sam and Matt had seen no shortage of those during their approach to town. Out by the creek that gave the town its name they'd seen placer miners aplenty shoveling dirt into crude sluice-boxes and using the creek's sluggish flow to filter whatever fine particles of gold or silver it might contain down to the bottom of their home-made 'rockers'.

Here in town, and that much closer to the western hills, of course, it was a different story. There was no room for small operators here. That's why all the big mining conglomerates had sent in their small armies; to buy up claims, sink shafts into the hills and send men down to dig whatever riches they could from out of the quartz below.

Those operations were clearly visible now, away to their right; shaft upon shaft pocking the slopes, half-hidden beneath wood or steel frames which carried the hoisting ropes upon which the men below depended, and laden pack-mules carrying mined ore up to the stream-powered stamp-mills on the ridges above, where it would be pounded down to yellow dust.

Somewhere up there they heard the muted thump of blasting-powder, and Sam cringed in the saddle. In their greed, the powers-that-be were digging their way ever deeper into those hills in their quest to find better, richer veins. Sam just hoped the whole damn' territory didn't cave in as a result of all their excavations.

He and Matt had to rein in at the first intersection they came to while a thick-bearded man led a slow-moving burro-train loaded down with mine-shoring timbers across their path, stalling just about every other form of transport on Main in the process.

It was as they were waiting for the last of the burros to clear the street that Sam hailed a big-bellied bear of a man sitting aboard a stalled freight-wagon beside them, and asked where he might find a lady by the name of Pearl Diamond.

The big man said he didn't have a clue, so Sam mentioned the fact that she was the wife of the local badge-packer, just to help jog his memory. Immediately the wagon-driver's square, reliable face darkened in expression.

'You mean Mrs. *Denton*,' he said.

Sam shrugged. 'I guess.'

'You kin or somethin'?'

'Not kin,' Sam replied honestly. 'But somethin' very much like it.'

'I sure hope so,' the wagon-driver growled fervently. ''Cause I figure that poor woman could use a friendly face right about now.'

Sam stiffened and a frown brought thin, gray-black brows down over his eyes. 'What's that supposed to mean?' he demanded.

Instead of replying, the wagon-driver used one blunt finger to indicate the woman's whereabouts. 'You'll find her at her house, little clapboard place halfway down the left-hand side of East Street,' he said.

But by now Sam had more on his mind than directions, and he wanted to find out why Pearl Denton — Pearl *Diamond*, as she'd been when he'd first met her — should be in need of a friend. 'Thanks, but tell me — '

Before he could say anything further, the burro-train passed out of sight and the wagon-driver kicked off the brake, slapped his own mules across the ass and began to rattle on up the street.

Sam watched him go, his frown still in place. After a moment he felt Matt's eyes on him. He met his partner's gaze, read the unspoken question within it and said, 'One way to find out, I guess.'

They turned left, onto East Street.

This thoroughfare was some wider

than Main, and not nearly so busy with traffic. Despite that, however, the character of the dwellings to either side of the muddy street stayed much the same; canvas tents standing alongside a fair number of small wooden cabins, many still being constructed.

Sam was quiet as they angled their horses toward their destination, a whitewashed clapboard structure still a few hundred feet away. Matt glanced across at his partner's grim profile and began to realize that this woman Pearl Denton, whose note had brought them all the way from Austin Springs, Colorado, meant more to Sam than Sam was letting on.

'Why don't you tell me about her?' Matt asked quietly.

Sam came up out of his reverie. 'Huh? What's that, boy?'

'Pearl. Tell me about her. *You* an' her.'

Sam shrugged. 'Not really all that much to tell,' he replied. 'You'll remember that, for a while back around

'70, '71, I bought a half-share in a joy-house down on the Barbary Coast. Nice place, real fancy. Champagne, chandeliers, the whole kit 'n' caboodle. Pearl was the girl we hired to run things — an' a right good job she made of it, too.

'She was a beautiful girl, Matt. Skin like satin, a figure like I don't know what. A real high-class lady. Had a good head for business, too. Made that little place of ours real profitable.

'But you know me. Never really took to the life. Wasn't a one for livin' off investments. Preferred to *earn* my money. So I gave it about six months, sold out to Pearl, moved on. Didn't miss it one bit. But Pearl there . . . ' His smile was brief and melancholy. 'Missed her more'n I could've said.'

Silence descended upon them, as the small whitewashed house drew closer on their left. Matt's next question was maybe a tad indelicate, but the boy was young, and still had much to learn about tact. 'Did you love her?' he asked softly.

If the question caused any offence, Sam didn't let it show. He stared moodily off into the distance, gray eyes narrowed to slits. Then he said, 'I don't know. Maybe. More likely I just cared for the *idea* of lovin' her.'

'And what about her? Pearl? How'd she feel about *you*?'

Sam threw him a bleak glance. 'Never got the chance to find out,' he replied brusquely. 'After I found her in bed with my partner one mornin', I didn't really deem it polite to ask.'

For just a second Matt saw a flash of pain in Sam's eyes. Then the older man returned his attention to the hazy distance. At once Matt realized that Sam had carried the hurt of that time around with him for more than ten years. Oh, he'd buried it well, sure; but Pearl's note, and the prospect of seeing her again, had brought it all back to the surface.

The revelation surprised him, for he'd always considered Sam to be a man of few secrets, and little sentimentality. Years before, back home in Brownwood, Texas, Matt had looked upon him as an adopted uncle. Hell, he guessed he still did. Sam had been his father's best friend. They'd been as fine a pair of Texas rangers as ever wore the star in the circle. Then pa had been killed at Cemetery Ridge in '63, and after the war Sam had left Texas for good and all to become a celebrated town-tamer alongside his friends Hickok and Stoudenmire.

It was only by chance that their trails had crossed once again, when Matt and a mismatched bunch of trail-wolves had decided to rob a bank in the very town where Sam had become marshal. Even now the memories of that time brought a sad furrow to Matt's brow, for he'd known some fine times with those other boys, whose lives had recently ended at the hands of the hangman. But some good had come of it all. He'd been reunited with that 'uncle' of his childhood, and the two of them had become good companions.

Still, there was something more to their relationship, yet another secret that Matt could not even begin to guess. Because Sam, the man he had always considered to be a close family friend, was in reality the man who had sired him. A momentary indiscretion with Bob Dury's wife, quickly over and bitterly regretted, had resulted in the whipcord-lean young man now riding alongside Sam. And now that Matt's ma, Rosie, had passed on, the secret was Sam's alone.

The older man had decided long ago that Matt would never learn the truth. Sam owed too much to Bob and Rosie to shatter the boy's memories of them. Still, Sam enjoyed the boy's company. He was bright, wise beyond his years in some things, altogether a real tonic for an ageing badge-packer who'd once been immortalized in a bunch of ten-cent libraries written by that womanizing jackanapes, Eddie Judson.

Sam settled himself more comfortably aboard his slow-moving roan. It had been a struggle, but eventually he and Matt had settled that business with the Austin Springs bank-robbers. But now Sam's mind was on Pearl Denton, and the nature of the trouble that had caused her to write for his help.

* * *

The clapboard house was small and neat. A few small but colorful flowers struggled for life in the hard Nevada soil to either side of the trimmed-timber front door.

Judge and Dury reined in before the house and sat their horses for what seemed like a long time before Sam finally swung down and passed his reins up to his partner.

He delved into his right-side saddle-bag, felt around for a moment, then lifted out a mottled tan-and-white ball of fur. This was Mitzi, his fat but nonetheless devoted Abyssinian cat.

24

The creature had simply wandered into Austin Springs about three years earlier and taken a shine to him. She had been a loyal fixture in his life ever since.

Now he set her down on the ground. 'Go stretch your legs for a while,' he said.

The cat meowed, yawned, blinked sleepy sea-green eyes at him and sauntered off.

Behind them, the hammering sounds of construction coming from a half-completed block of cabins across the street blended with the jarring thump of the stamp-mills. In the distance they heard another dull crash of blasting-powder being detonated deep inside the hills to the west. Earlier, a rare but heavy shower had turned King Creek's streets to mud, but now that the sun had come back out, the ground had started to steam itself dry.

Matt looked down at the older man, whose mild, gunmetal-gray eyes were now moving slowly across the tar-paper windows of the clapboard house, trying to see beyond the thick lace curtains. Beneath his battered old Stetson, Sam's expression appeared strangely reluctant, as if he'd have preferred to remount, turn around and ride away.

Before he could do any such thing, however, Matt attempted to lighten his mood. 'You gonna stand there all day, Sam?'

'Huh?'

'Only I'm kind of anxious to see this real high-class lady you been tellin' me about. You remember; the one with the skin like satin and the figure like you don't know what — '

Sam offered him a sour look. 'Very funny,' he growled.

Wiping his palms on the back pockets of his gray duck pants, he took one uncertain pace forward, then another. Three more and he was at the front door, just about to rap at the unfinished wood and announce himself, when three sounds suddenly issued from within.

A shattering of glass.

A deep, masculine roar.

And then the awful, deafening boom of a shotgun.

2

As soon as he'd pinpointed the location of the gun blast, Sam wheeled around and yelled, 'Out back — *quick!*'

Still mounted some yards away, Matt released his grip on Sam's reins, trusting the older man's horse to stay put, then jammed his heels into his pony's flanks and shot off down the narrow alley between Pearl Denton's house and the smaller cabin next door.

Not that Sam wasted any time in watching him go. Again his Remington seemed to leap into his palm as he spun back to slam his left shoulder against the front door.

At first the door refused to give. Bouncing off the stubborn wood and swearing under his breath at the pain his efforts had brought him, he threw his weight at it again. This time he heard a splintering crack as the door shuddered inwards.

The room into which he blundered was neat, with a low ceiling and three home-made rugs tossed across the swept-earth floor. His busy eyes didn't miss a thing. He saw a couple of easy chairs beside a cold hearth, a table, four ladderbacks, a few cupboards, a pie safe, a copper sink and a pile of stacked dishes.

But no people, alive or otherwise.

There was a door in the facing wall. Sam crossed over to it, sucked in a deep breath and threw it open.

He found himself on the threshold of a small, gloomy bedroom. He saw a double bed with a trunk at its foot, a bedside cupboard with an ashtray overspilling with crushed butts. Directly across from him was a window, half-hidden by gently shifting drapes. A shattered window.

It was in that moment that he also saw the man in the bed.

The man who was pointing a riot gun at him.

Sam yelled, '*Hell, no!*'

The man said, 'Hell, *yes!*'

And the riot gun just went *boom!* again.

But by then Sam had hauled ass back into the parlor, slamming the door behind him. He threw himself to one side just as the shotgun pellets ventilated the wood.

Outside he caught a few confused shouts that mingled with the pounding of horses' hooves. The words were muffled and didn't mean much. Then Sam heard the high, wicked crack of a pistol, once, twice, a whole flurry of shots, and knew he couldn't spend the rest of the day just leaning up against the parlor wall.

When at last he moved he did so with a speed that was pretty good for a man just four years off fifty. He booted the bedroom door open and went in with the Remington aimed at the man in the bed.

'*Hold it!*' he barked, and the man in the bed, who looked to be of a similar age but not nearly as spry, froze in the act of reloading the Greener.

They locked stares for a moment. The man in the bed was sweating hard and had sick, tired eyes. As hard as it seemed to believe, Sam guessed he must be Pearl's old man — the marshal of King Creek. He indicated the shotgun and said, 'We'll have no more of that, Denton. Believe it or not, I'm on your side.'

Another pair of high, whiny gunshots made them both turn their attention to the shattered window. Sam hurried across to it, crunching shards of glass underfoot, and pushed the jagged frame open.

The movement caused a few remaining fragments to fall out and land with a musical tinkle on two paint cans which had been discarded just beneath the window-sill. One of them had a length of thin gray rope coiled around it. Not far away, Sam saw a red stain soaking slowly into the dirt.

Blood.

Cautiously he poked his head outside and glanced both ways. The land out back of the cabins and tents that made up this side of East Street rose slowly toward a straggly line of brush and trees eighty feet away. From the looks of it, most folks used the area as a dumping-ground for their trash. Here and there amid the piles of junk stood a few tall wooden outhouses, but that was all.

About thirty yards away, Matt's pony stood ground-reined, head bent and chewing at some sparse greenery. Not far from the animal, Matt was kneeling beside a man sprawled on his back, inspecting the fellow's crimson chest.

Sam threw a glance back into the room, just to make sure Denton hadn't had any second thoughts about reloading the Greener. The man lay where he was, his big, rugged face pale and slack.

'I'll be back directly,' Sam told him sharply. 'Somethin's happened out there, but I'm damned if I know what.'

'Did you . . . did you get 'em?' Denton husked.

Sam shrugged. 'We got *someone*.'

He climbed out the window and trotted up to Matt, keeping his gun in hand and his eyes vigilant. Only when he reached his companion and was fairly certain there'd be no further trouble did he slip the Remington back into leather and hunker down to study the body.

Whoever he was, he'd sure been punctured permanent. He'd been about twenty-six, twenty-eight, with thick brown hair and a beard of matching hue. His eyes were glassy, his pupils dilated, his nose sharp and in need of a blow. His mouth was open to reveal slowly rotting teeth and his shirt bore a nasty splash of claret where Matt's bullet had knocked all the life out of him. About the saddest thing of all, though, was the look of surprise on the dead man's face; as if the poor bastard just couldn't believe his own mortality.

Sam glanced across at Matt. The younger man handled both his sidearms with near-equal proficiency. He'd taken life with them once before. But death, sudden or otherwise, still shocked him. His face was almost as bloodless as that of the man on the ground, and his gray eyes had taken on a haunted look.

Sam said, 'What happened?'

Matt focused on the older man and licked his lips. 'Came around back, like you said. Saw a pair of fellers near yonder window. One had just caught an arm full of pellets an' was howlin' like a wolf. He was makin' for two horses they had ground-hitched just back there a ways. When they saw me, this one threw down whatever it was he was heftin' . . . what was it?' He squinted back the way he'd come. 'Paint cans?'

'Yeah. Go on.'

'Well, he drew iron an' we exchanged shots. His partner got aboard his horse an' lit out. This feller's mount just followed on, trippin' an' stumblin', real wild, so I . . . I . . . ' His voice dried up.

'You did the right thing,' Sam finished firmly. 'That's what you did.'

'But . . . paint cans, Sam? What in

hell's name is this all about?'

Sam shrugged. 'Lord knows. But I sure intend to find out.'

With as much detachment as he could muster, Sam quickly went through the dead man's pockets. He found ten dollars in bills, three dollars in change, a fairly lewd French postcard and a letter from Hays, Kansas, identifying the deceased as Benjamin Joseph Weeks.

He also found a thin copper spoon, which he frowned at, then pocketed.

Together he and Matt straightened up. A few women had appeared at their back doors to see what was going on, and some of the construction workers from across the street, drawn by all the gunfire, filled the far end of the alley. Ignoring them, Sam started back towards the Denton house with Matt in tow.

When they were close enough, Sam called out, 'Denton! Hold your fire. We're comin' in!'

There was a pause. Then Denton

said, 'Come ahead.'

Crunching more broken glass to powder, they climbed back through the window to confront the man in the bed. Beneath the sheets, Denton looked like a tall man. Chances were he'd been a blocky sonofabitch in his time, too. But whatever illness had confined him to bed had also whittled him down to little more than a skeleton. He had a lumpy, pale face, dark, intelligent eyes, black hair strewn across his lined forehead and a pale blue shadow sketching his lantern jaw.

He looked up at Sam, the shotgun still clutched in his right hand but aimed at no-one in particular, his left using a kerchief to mop his shining face. From what they could see of him, he was wearing only a pair of faded combinations. 'You'll be Judge,' he said in a lifeless, phlegm-choked voice. 'The one Pearl sent for.'

Sam nodded. 'Yeah, I'm Judge. And this here's my partner, Matt Dury.'

Denton glanced across at Matt, then

let his rheumy eyes shuttle over to the ruined bedroom door. 'Sorry about that,' he said to Sam. 'Thought you was with them, at first.'

Sam said, 'Forget it. But tell me somethin'.'

'Name it.'

'Who wants you dead, Denton? And why?'

The man in the bed was just about to reply when his attention was taken by the sound of a horse pounding to a halt out front, and, a moment later, heavy footsteps clattering across the parlor floor. A voice called out, 'Denton? Jack? You all right in there?'

The newcomer came to a halt in the bedroom doorway, holding a .38 caliber New Line Police Colt in his left hand. He eyed Denton briefly, just to make sure he was still breathing, then treated Sam and Matt to a longer, more suspicious scrutiny.

'Well, well, well,' he said. 'What have we got here?'

He was a biggish man, thirty or so,

thick in the chest and fairly shoe-horned into his gray town suit. He stood just under six feet in height and had short, tobacco-colored hair spilling out from beneath his gray beaver hat. His brow and lips were thick and pronounced, his eyes brown, bright and shrewd, and his nose was long, once broken but neatly fixed. He wore a cheap tin shield pinned on his right lapel and he had a deep, ponderous voice with a strong midwestern accent.

'Don't get your bowels in an uproar, Dick,' Denton said tiredly. 'There was some trouble here. Thanks to these fellers, it wasn't as bad as it might've been.'

The deputy raised one eyebrow, keeping his gaze on Sam. 'Oh?' The suspicion refused to leave his tone. 'And who might you be?'

Sam said, 'Friends of the family.' Then he gave the deputy their names.

The deputy said, 'Sam Judge? Are you kidding me, mister? 'Cause if you are, I don't find it at all amusing. Sam

Judge's just a figure in the dime novels. The one who took on Six-Knife Solomon and all them other barmen that never really existed.'

'I'm Judge, all right,' Sam insisted quietly, irritated by the newcomer's manner. 'Now, why don't you tell us who *you* are?'

It was the deputy's turn to bristle, but he held back from snapping a retort. 'The name's Whiteley,' he said instead. 'Dick Whiteley, acting marshal of King Creek while Jack here's on sick leave.'

Sam nodded in understanding. 'Well, then, *marshal*, I guess we'd better make a statement.'

Whiteley reholstered his gun in a shoulder rig and said, 'Yeah — I guess you better had.'

Briefly Sam recounted the events which had led to the death of Benjamin Joseph Weeks and the wounding of his unknown accomplice. Whiteley listened without noticeable interest. Then he climbed out back, inspected the body, checked the deceased's handgun, grudgingly agreed that Matt had acted in self-defense, told the rubberneckers to go about their business before he arrested them for obstruction, then returned to the bedroom.

'You heard this feller Weeks and his companion skulking around out back, did you?' Whiteley asked, addressing Denton.

The man in the bed nodded. He looked plumb tuckered, too tired to waste whatever energy he had left on words.

'And you just opened up on 'em,' the acting marshal prodded, indicating the now broken-open shotgun. 'With that thing?'

'It seemed like the thing to do.'

Whiteley shook his head and made a few soft tut-tutting sounds to signify that he was not a happy man. 'I don't like the sound of that, Jack. I mean, I know you must feel a little, well, uh, *vulnerable* after what them other fellers did to you, but you can't just go around shooting at everyone you *think* might be up to no good.'

Denton used his left hand to indicate his withered body. 'I can't go around *anywhere*, Dick.'

'That's beside the point,' Whiteley replied. 'What I'm saying is, if this other *hombre*, the one you wounded, was to come forward and press charges, it'd go bad for you, Jack. I mean, it's not even as if you started shooting in self-defense. The way *I* understand it, these fellers was just walking past when you took it into your head to get *them* before they *got you*.'

'Oh, Denton acted in defense of his life all right,' Sam interrupted.

Whiteley turned to face him. 'How so?'

'You notice those paint cans just outside the window?'

The acting marshal nodded.

'Well, lessen I miss my guess, you open 'em up and you'll find 'em brim-full with blastin'-powder.'

'*What?*'

'You heard. There's some thin gray rope coiled around one of the cans. At first I figured it for twine. Now I'd say it's more likely a length of Bickford Safety Fuse.'

Whiteley's heavy-browed face registered surprise, but some lawman's instinct gave Sam the impression that he wasn't telling Whiteley anything he didn't already know. Regardless however, he went on.

'What finally clinched it was this,' he said, taking the long, thin copper spoon from his pocket. 'I took it off the dead man while I was checkin' him over for ID. In case you don't know it, Whiteley, it's the kind of spoon a blasting-engineer uses when he's handlin' black powder. Copper tools — or wood, come to that — don't spark like iron ones. And a spark's the last thing you want when you're handlin' explosives.'

Matt muttered, '*Judas* . . . ' and Denton's haggard face took on fresh lines of worry. But Whiteley, taking the spoon and examining it more for something to do than anything else, just remained noncommittal.

Finally he eyed Denton. 'You got any reason to believe anyone'd want you murdered, Jack?' he enquired.

Denton's smile was short-lived, more a bitter twist of the lips. 'I think you already know the answer to that, *marshal*.'

Whiteley ignored the sarcasm. 'All right,' he sighed. 'Smart figuring, Judge, I'll grant you that. But when you boil it down, all we've really got is a mess of speculation. I mean, what's to say these two fellers you claim was after blowing Jack here to perdition wasn't just a couple of blasting-engineers taking their powder on up to the mines?'

'Why don't you find the one who got away an' ask him?' Matt suggested mildly. 'He had an arm full of 00 buckshot last time I saw 'im. Shouldn't be difficult to spot.'

Whiteley clearly did not like being advised by a younger man. 'Every doctor working in this town has orders to report gunshot wounds to me,' he said. 'If this particular feller seeks medical treatment, I'll get to hear about it.'

'Well, let's hope it's sooner rather than later,' Sam growled.

Whiteley made a few busy-busy gestures as he slipped the copper spoon into his inside jacket pocket. 'Well, I'd better get along. I got to get the body picked up, have someone bring them paint cans in . . . '

'Sure,' said Denton, waving him away.

'Well . . . try not to fret too much, Jack. We'll get it all sorted out.'

Whiteley nodded his farewells and left the house. A moment later they heard the drumming of his horse's hooves fading back towards Main.

Sam broke the silence. 'Well,' he said. 'Feel like openin' up now, Denton? What *is* all this about, an' who exactly put you in that sick-bed?'

Denton looked up at him. 'Sick-bed?'

he echoed. 'This isn't a sick-bed, Judge, it's a *death-bed*! Damn them . . . they'll stop at nothing, the bastards . . . Blasting-powder, for heaven's sake!' Suddenly his eyes flooded with tears and Matt shuffled his feet uncomfortably. 'If Pearl'd been here instead of out marketing,' the King Creek marshal whispered in a broken voice. 'If anything had happened to her because of me . . . Oh God . . . '

He started to cry.

Sam glanced over at his companion, feeling equally powerless to comfort the man in the bed. 'Go take care of the horses, Matt,' he sighed quietly. 'I'll fix up a pot of coffee. I got a feelin' this is gonna be a lo-o-ong day.'

* * *

While Matt took the horses around back, loosened their cinches and hitched them to Pearl Denton's empty clothes-line, Sam brewed up a pot of good strong coffee. By the time he took a mug in to Pearl's bedridden husband, however, Jack Denton had fallen into a deep sleep. The unloaded Greener was still clutched in his right hand.

Sam looked down at the man's rugged face, wondering just what in hell really *was* happening here. He glanced over at the ruined window. Glass being in somewhat short supply in such uncivilized parts, he'd have to scare up some plywood and board the window up temporarily. But that was a job for later — once he and Matt finally got the answers they had coming.

Returning to the parlor, he found Matt sitting at the table and gave him the mug he'd been intending to give Denton. His own coffee was black and sweet, strong enough to float a horse-shoe.

They drank in silence. There wasn't a whole lot else they could do now but wait for Pearl to come home from the stores. While they waited, the local undertaker and his apprentice drew up out front in a plain, open-backed light wagon and collected the body and the blasting-powder with surprising good cheer.

About three-quarters of an hour later they heard footsteps outside, then a small, feminine gasp as whoever was out there — almost certainly Pearl — noticed the front door's shattered lock. Sam was over to the door in a trice, opening it fast so that he could set the woman's mind at ease before she started to think the worst.

But the woman with whom he came face to face wasn't Pearl. This woman was around the mid-forties, five feet seven, and damn' near as broad as she was tall. Her two hundred pounds were squeezed into a too-tight dress of some faded but flowery design, so that at first she appeared to be all breasts and belly. Then he looked at her face, saw piggy but kind green eyes, a smallish, upturned nose and heart-shaped lips pressed into a pout by heavy, trembling cheeks. Her make-up was a bit gaudy — evening-blue eye-shadow, rouged cheeks and scarlet lips — and her chestnut-brown hair was piled up in a spill of tight curls, but she seemed like a decent-enough type.

Sam said, 'Uh . . . howdy, ma'am. Can I help you?'

And the woman said, 'Sam?'

Startled, he froze there in the doorway with his gray eyes narrowed. After a moment he said, '*Pearl?*'

By way of reply she said, 'Oh, Sam!' and dropped her little bag of groceries so that she could step in close and hug him.

Sam hugged her back, still shocked by the change that had come over the once sylph-like bawdy-house madam. The last ten years had sure been a little less than kind to her, but maybe that's how life treated you when you got out of a profitable business and married up with a lawman. A moment passed, then he held her at arms' length, just to make sure it really *was* Pearl he'd been holding and not her grandmother, and finally he recognized a trace of the

48

younger Pearl in this beefier woman's face.

'Good to see you, Pearl,' he said softly and sincerely.

Her green eyes sparkled moistly. 'You too, Sam. I'm . . . I'm right sorry for writin' to you the way I did . . . I . . . I just couldn't think of anyone else who could get us *out* of this fix.'

'And what 'fix' is that?' he asked.

Her eyes travelled down to the shattered lock. 'What — ?'

'It's all right,' he said, reaching down to scoop up her groceries. 'There was a donnybrook of sorts here about an hour so ago, but it's all over now.'

Beneath her make-up, she blanched. 'Jack — ?'

'Sleepin' like a baby,' Sam told her, taking her by one chubby arm and ushering her inside. 'So don't fret.' In a few terse sentences he told her everything that had happened.

As soon as he was through she hurried across the room and disappeared into the bedroom. He heard her small gasp of surprise as she saw the state of the bedroom window, listened to the silence as she lumbered around the bed to peer down at her sick, sleeping husband, felt his jaw-muscles shifting with suppressed fury when she began to sob quietly, and clenched his fists.

A moment later she came back out, dabbing at her now-sore eyes. There was so much sorrow in this house that it seemed impossible to imagine that a girl who'd known so many good times could ever have ended up this way. She looked up into Sam's lean, lined face and her bottom lip quivered dangerously.

'Oh, Sam — ' she choked.

He held her again, as more sobs racked her obese frame. At last she stopped crying and relaxed, exhausted by emotion as most folks are after a good weep. Then he cleared his throat and indicated a chair.

'Come along now, Pearl. Take the weight off.' Mentally he bit his tongue.

'And tell us what all this is about.'

She stiffened. 'Us?'

He realized she hadn't even noticed Matt, sitting at the table. Now the youngster stood up and came forward, offering his hand while Sam introduced him. She mumbled something, another apology, and Matt waved it away gallantly. 'Forget it,' he said politely. 'Come an' sit down, ma'am. Here, let me get you a cup of coffee.'

Sam watched his son go over to the range and busy himself with the pot and a cup, feeling a sudden rush of pride in the boy. He felt Pearl's eyes on him and glanced down at her. There was a question in her expression that he found uncomfortable, almost as if she'd seen a likeness in them both and guessed the truth. But all she said was, 'Thanks, Sam . . . thanks *both* of you . . . for comin' . . . '

They got her settled down at the table and joined her. Sam asked if he could smoke and she told him to go ahead. He promptly took out one of the noxious three-for-a-dime cigars Matt had learned to detest and lit up. Soon a hazy gray cloud of smoke hung around the Rochester lamp suspended over the table.

'All right,' Sam said around the stogie. 'We're listenin'.'

'Well,' she said, laughing a bit self-consciously. 'It's kind of difficult to know where to start. I had it all planned out, y'see, but I guess comin' home and findin' you already here, and hearin' about this trouble out back . . . '

She shook her head as if to clear it and took a pull at her coffee. 'No matter. I'll just jaw and you two can pull the bones out of it.'

'Fair enough.'

She brought order to her thoughts, then said, 'About ten months ago a couple fellers discovered traces of gold out by the creek and up in the hills. Assay office over to Stillwater checked out the samples and found 'em to be the stuff bonanzas're made of.

'Pretty soon King Creek was overrun

by speculators, some lucky, some not so lucky.

'Well, you've packed a badge for long enough, Sam; I don't need to tell you that for every feller who struck it rich, twenty more had come to town to relieve him of his cash. Sportin' girls, crooked games of chance, overpriced and watered-down drinks. There's no end to the way some folks'll try to gyp others.

'Soon the miners started turnin' ugly. There was a lynchin' out by the south end of town, some fool tinhorn usin' marked cards. So a few civic-minded gents got together and decided to hire some law before things got completely out of control.'

'Jack,' Sam guessed.

Pearl nodded again, lifting her steaming cup. 'We was livin' over to Carson City at the time. Jack was workin' as a deputy at the courthouse. But the money King Creek was offerin' was so good that we just upped stakes and came here to live. Jack hired on a deputy, Dick Whiteley, and they set about cleanin' King Creek up.'

Her expression turned wistful. 'It was tough, at first. I declare, that husband of mine worked eighteen hours a day to bring order to them streets. Did a good job, too. But then . . . ' Her face clouded over. 'But then,' she said, 'the Stovers came to town.'

Matt sat up straight. 'Stover? That's the name of the feller we had that little run-in with this mornin'.'

Pearl glanced across at Sam. 'Run-in?' she asked. Sam told her all about it. 'Ah, that'll be Randolph,' she said when he'd finished.

'I disremember the Christian name,' Sam replied. 'But you say there's *more* of these Stovers?'

'Three more,' Pearl nodded. 'Randolph's two brothers, Dale and Gene, and their mama, Kate. And let me tell you boys; never did such a cold-hearted bitch give birth to three more vicious dogs.'

★　★　★

Matt smiled across at the fat woman. 'I could be wrong,' he said drily, 'but I get the feelin' you don't much care for these Stovers.'

She returned the smile and Sam, studying her profile, was reminded just a little of the woman she used to be. When she stopped smiling, however, sadness found itself battling bitterness in her small green eyes.

'Let me tell you boys somethin',' she said soberly. 'You can forget everythin' else you've ever heard about the kind of vultures who work the gold camps of the west. The Stovers have turned all the gyppin' and petty-thievery into a fine art. They're ruthless, and they'll stop at nothin' to bleed these poor miners dry, because, like I say, the stakes are high. The country around these parts is *that* rich in precious metals.'

She finished her coffee. 'Furthermore,' she continued, 'the Stovers don't just want a slice of the pie. They want the whole damn' thing, and they're not fussy as to how they get it. Merchants sellin' the self-same goods as Randolph, but for half the price, have turned up dead or missin'. Saloons that rival Dale's *Pot of Gold* and refuse to pay him what he calls a 'concession', have mysteriously burned to the ground. Had a freight-line here once that set up against the haulage business young Gene operates. Owner was run out of town one night, for no good reason. He never came back.'

She sighed. 'You want me to go on? All right. They employ about a dozen thugs to operate their protection racket. They sell moonshine colored with caramel over at the *Pot of Gold* that's so strong it's been known to send men into convulsions, and temporarily blind more'n a few. Old Kate directs everythin'. She sits up in that fine house they've had built on Crane Rock and spends her every day pullin' the strings that make the rest of King Creek dance.'

Sam digested all that she had said. 'What do you know of these Stovers?' he asked.

'Only what Jack found out when he started makin' enquiries about 'em,' Pearl replied. 'They hail from Delorane, Wisconsin. Evidently Kate's husband was a somewhat reckless stockbroker. Died about seven years ago and left 'em with nary a penny, so they set about makin' a fortune of their own.' Seeing Matt's questioning look, she explained, 'It appears that the Stovers've got quite a history of fleecin' the gold camps up and down the country. Only this time, like I say, they're playin' that much harder.

'Jack saw what was happenin', of course,' she continued. 'It's just not possible to come in and take over a whole town on the q.t. He heard so many stories about the Stovers and their intimidation tactics that he just *had* to go on up there and tell 'em to desist or face the consequences.

'But they paid him no mind. Just went right on with all their bully-boy antics until he had no choice but to threaten to call in a U.S. Marshal.'

She fell silent for a moment, and bowed her head.

'I don't know whether Jack really did spook them Stovers, or whether they just decided to make him an example to everyone else,' she went on. 'Whichever it was — they had someone cut him down with a shotgun one dark night about a month ago.' Her green eyes glistened. 'Left him for dead,' she explained. 'But he pulled through. Buckshot shattered his left hip and pelvis . . . doctor doubts he'll ever walk again . . . but . . . but he'll live, Sam — provided the Stovers don't get lucky and manage to finish the job once and for all.'

Sam swore softly as everything that had occurred there earlier began to make sense. 'This deputy,' he said. 'Whiteley. What'd *he* do about findin' the feller that cut Jack down?'

Pearl gave a short, grim laugh. 'You met him,' she said. 'What do *you* think?'

'Nothin',' Sam replied.

'Right,' she confirmed. 'And for a

very good reason, too. *Because Jack is almost certain it was Dick Whiteley who pulled the trigger on him.*'

'I *knew* there was somethin' crooked about that sorry-lookin' sonofabitch!' Sam hissed angrily. He gave the matter some thought. 'You sure are in a hell of a jam,' he decided, flicking ash into the saucer in the centre of the table. 'But I don't see that there's much I can do about it, Pearl. Leastways not as a civilian.' He squinted at her. 'Suppose we was to go ahead an' call in a U.S. Marshal?'

'Easier said than done,' Pearl replied. 'First of all, the nearest Western Union office is in Dalhart, which is about eighty miles south-east. If the Stovers are keepin' a watch on things, as I suspicion they *are*, I doubt you'd ever get there alive. And even if you *did*, what's to say that your wire to the U.S. Marshal's office in Reno would actually get *through*.'

Matt said, 'Looks like we're on our own, then.'

'These 'civic-minded gents' you spoke of,' said Sam. 'What are they, the town council?'

'Pretty much. The folks in these parts are too busy diggin' to bother with formal elections, so they just went ahead and elected themselves.'

Sam reached a decision. 'All right. See if you can get 'em together here tonight, say around seven.'

The sudden glimmer of hope in Pearl's voice was almost pitiful. 'You've got a notion?' she asked quietly.

'Of sorts,' he replied. 'I'm gonna put it to 'em that they should pass a vote of no confidence in Dick Whiteley. Then, once he's out of the way, *I'll* pin on their badge of office.' He offered the woman a smile of comfort. 'Now take that worried look off your face, Pearl. Just as soon as I've got the clout, I'll be settlin' matters with these here Stovers once an' for all — I promise.'

3

When it got too dark for the placer miners to work, and the men toiling down in the lamp-lit shafts to the west finally ended their shifts, the saloons and brothels and gambling-dens readied themselves for another night's hoot 'n' holler.

Tonight was no different.

Yet.

The streets, busy all day, grew even busier as the miners came in from the outskirts of town. They came to patronize the eateries and bath-houses, to drop off their laundry and go grab themselves some fun. They came in wagons, aboard sway-backed mules and horses, or just plain afoot. They looked exhausted but optimistic, good-natured for the most part, and eager to forget the day's back-breaking exertions for a few hours.

Soon the air came alive with pianos and sporadic, drunken gunshots. Whores laughed gaily and glasses clinked in toast. Somewhere a woman sang, beautifully. On the other side of town a fight broke out and ended in a near-fatal stabbing.

Down at his general store, Randolph Stover threw one last look along his well-stocked shelves, at the neatly-stacked sacks of sugar, salt and flour, the jars of molasses and plum preserves, the tin crockery, ammunition, tobacco, airtights, playing-cards, red and blue flannel shirts and belt-knives. He saw bolts of cloth, one-pound bars of Castile and lye soap, sweetmeats, linen thread, cured pork, preserved potatoes, dried vegetables and pemmican. His flinty brown eyes finally came to rest on the well-stocked cracker barrel in the far corner and his surly mouth twitched into something like a smile of satisfaction.

It had been a good day's trading. He hadn't shifted much stock, but at the prices he charged, he didn't need to. Coltrain had taken the day's takings — five hundred dollars — on ahead, for Mother to deposit in the cast-iron Jenks & Millbush safe at home. Randolph had sent Baker along with him, for extra security.

Randolph stroked his handlebar moustache thoughtfully as he scanned the room one last time. Yes, all was as it should be. The door to the storeroom was locked and bolted. It only remained for him to padlock the front door, then he could take a slow stroll home, perhaps stop off at the *Pot of Gold* for a medicinal and an hour or so with one of those beautiful blondes Dale had brought in from Virginia City.

Randolph untied his apron, shrugged out of it, draped it across the stool behind the counter and took his gray suit jacket down from the peg in the wall. He slipped into the jacket, enjoying the feel of the fine material and the snugness of its hand-tailored fit, then rearranged his sky-blue cravat and tugged at his red vest. At last he was ready. He took out a large gold turnip watch, checked the time. Eight o'clock, dead on.

One by one he turned out the kerosene lamps hanging from the low rafters, adhering to the custom he had established during the short time he and Mother and his brothers had been in town. At the door he trimmed the final lamp, throwing the store into darkness.

He stepped out onto the boardwalk, the sound of his footsteps loud in the relative peace which had descended upon this part of town. He locked up, padlocked the front door, checked the chain with a couple of sharp tugs, then turned to face the street.

As he peered up and down Main, he suddenly found himself thinking about the two men who'd bought into that business with Harrigan earlier on, the old man and the boy. Again he wondered who they were. Coltrain and

Baker were still furious with them, and he could hardly blame them. Perhaps he would tell them to make a few enquiries, discover the identities of these meddlesome newcomers. Just in case . . .

He dug into an inside pocket and fished out a long, fat Cuban cigar. He bit off one end and spat it out. With the cigar clamped in his mouth, he searched for his matches, found them, took one out, scratched it to life —

★   ★   ★

The figure loitering in the shadows of the narrow alleyway directly opposite the store stiffened as his target struck the match. A tingle washed through him, and his grip on the Martini-Henry rifle in his clammy hands increased.

For just a moment Randolph's face was splashed with uncertain yellow light. The rifleman saw him clearly. He swallowed hard, not at all sure now that he could go through with his self-appointed task.

But then —

Dammit! This was no time for self-doubt, and certainly no time for further thought. Lord knew, he'd spent enough time thinking this thing through as it was! Slapping the Martini-Henry to his shoulder, he aimed at the small, flickering pinprick of light and squeezed the British rifle's trigger.

The gun blast was loud, but just one more sound in the night busy with noise. The .402 caliber bullet struck Randolph square in the face and exited the back of his head in a veritable shower of dark-red meat. He was most probably dead within seconds.

The rifleman watched him collapse to the boardwalk, then turned and hurried away from the scene of the murder. His mind was in turmoil. He wanted to be sick. He wanted to turn the clock back and give the dead man a reprieve. And yet, at the same time, he wanted to yell aloud his exultation at having removed the one obstacle between him and power.

His horse was tethered just a short distance from here. He would be mounted within moments, and on his way back home. He was thinking that when, reaching the far end of the alley, he turned the corner and barreled straight into someone coming at him from the opposite direction.

For a moment there was confusion in the dark, confining space at the end of the narrow avenue, and a few grunts of surprise. Then the newcomer, a short, wrinkled little man with a drinker's nose and thinning, iron-gray hair beneath his sweat-stained sandy hat, peered through the gloom at the man holding the rifle.

'B-b-beg your par — why, i-i-it's Mr — '

Cursing inwardly, the rifleman raised one palm for silence, trying to keep the Martini-Henry held low down by his right leg, out of sight in the darkness. 'MacLean,' he said, forcing his tone to remain even. 'You, ah, you gave me a start.'

The other man, Tom MacLean, had been a blasting-engineer up until 1877, when his employers had given him some newfangled nitroglycerine to work with instead of the usual black powder. A premature explosion had robbed him of his confidence as well as his right arm. These days he followed the mining companies from town to town, working at any kind of odd jobs to earn enough money to keep himself under the influence of *Vin Vitae*.

For a moment there was an awkward silence between them. MacLean had seen his rifle, the killer felt sure. But there was some talk that the explosion which had ended the man's blasting career had also addled his brain. Certainly it had slurred his speech.

It finally dawned upon the killer that the situation might not be as bad as he'd first thought.

'Y-y-you, ah . . . f-f-feelin' all r-r-right?' MacLean asked. In the dim gray light of the alley he had curious, glassy gray eyes, a round, weak chin, a slack, open mouth. The rifleman could smell the tonic coming off his breath in waves. 'Y-y-you look kinda sh-shook up, iffen you d-d-don't mind me m-m-mentionin' it, Mr — '

'I'm fine,' the rifleman snapped. 'You, ah, you startled me is all.' He paused. 'Headed anyplace special?'

MacLean suddenly remembered his destination. He mumbled a response.

The rifleman frowned, relieved that his heart had stopped hammering at last. 'What was that?'

'D-d-druggist,' MacLean repeated, not meeting his gaze. 'M h-headin' for the d-drugst-store.'

The rifleman nodded. He'd already guessed as much. MacLean was a frequent visitor to King Creek's two apothecaries. They were the only places at which he could buy his euphoria-inducing tonic.

'Better hustle, then,' the rifleman advised. 'They'll be closing soon.'

MacLean bobbed his shabby head as

a look of panic entered his bloodshot eyes. 'Uh . . . y-yeah, tha's right!'

'Here.' The rifleman produced a five-dollar bill. 'Have this one on me.' He forced a smile.

MacLean stared at the bill a moment, then reached up and folded his left hand around it. 'Why, th-thanks, Mr — '

'Don't mention it,' the rifleman replied, holding MacLean's stare and speaking very deliberately so that the one-time blasting-engineer could not possibly miss the meaning of his next words. 'It's important to know who your friends are, Tom. Me, I'll always be good for a couple of dollars if ever you need them.'

MacLean's surprise was obvious. Before this meeting, he and his new-found benefactor had passed the time of day perhaps twice, no more. 'Ob-b-bliged,' MacLean said. His eyes shuttled to a point somewhere beyond the rifleman's right shoulder. 'Uh, listen, I gotta g-go . . . '

'Sure. So long.'

He watched MacLean hustle off, wondering if the man could be trusted to keep his mouth shut. Chances were that the blasting-engineer would remember little of their meeting by tomorrow morning. He'd probably spend most of the day sleeping off tonight's jag.

Still, he would have to be watched — closely — until this business with Randolph blew over. After all, the rifleman had no particular desire to die choking at the end of a rope. Especially for the murder of one so worthless.

*   *   *

Dick Whiteley looked up as the law office door swung open.

Pale, watery dawn light dribbled in through the small, barred windows to either side of the portal, illuminating a fair-sized room with plank walls covered in dodgers. A large, spur-scratched desk sat in the centre of the room.

Whiteley sat behind it in a sturdy-looking Douglas chair. Behind Whiteley rose a wall of thick iron bars. Beyond the bars lay a large cell with one set of bunk beds affixed to each of the opposing walls.

At the moment, the communal cell was empty.

Whiteley squinted at the newcomers through bleary brown eyes. Beyond the door, Main Street was already bustling, and the deadening *thump-thump* of the stamp-mills carried clearly from the jagged western slopes.

Two men entered his office. A fat tan-and-white cat followed them in. By the time the younger of the two closed the door behind them, Whiteley had put names to the faces.

'It's Judge, isn't it?' he said. 'Judge and Dury. And a cat.'

'Called Mitzi,' Sam nodded, inspecting the office with a critical eye. A black, pot-bellied stove squatted to the left of Whiteley's desk, atop which was perched a blue enamel coffee-pot. On the other side of the room stretched a lumpy horsehair sofa. Sam went over to the stove, helped himself to two mugs, blew in them to shift the dust and poured coffee. Whiteley watched him with a trace of anger tightening his face. Idly he noticed that the little finger on Sam's right hand was missing.

'Make yourself at home, why don't you?' he said sarcastically.

'Thanks,' Sam replied. 'I will.' He smiled briefly as he passed a mug to his companion, but by the time he'd returned his attention to Whiteley, his expression had grown hard once again. 'Oh, an' while we're talkin' 'bout takin' liberties, Whiteley . . . you're sittin' in my chair.'

Whiteley's heavy-boned face looked blank for a moment, until a frown lowered his brow. 'How's that again?'

'You mean you haven't seen this mornin's *Clarion* yet?'

'I been too busy working my gonads off for . . . ' The acting lawman paused to eye Sam shrewdly. His jacket was

73

draped over the back of the chair and his beaver hat hung on a nail in back of the door. The sleeves of his creased nankeen shirt were rolled up to reveal his meaty arms, and he had removed his celluloid collar. His .38 still hung in its holster beneath his right armpit, however. He looked pale and drawn, and his neatly-clipped brown hair was mussed. From the look of one of the bunks inside the cell, he hadn't bothered going home the night before. 'What's the *Clarion* got to do with anything?' he asked.

Sam took a copy of the single-sheet newspaper from the inside pocket of his buckskin jacket and held it out. The headline told the crooked deputy all he needed to know.

'You're a rotten apple, Whiteley,' Sam said bluntly. 'You know it. The town council knows it. And they want you out of here, fast, before you can spoil anything else.'

Whiteley scanned the sheet with something like disbelief mixing with outrage on his face. 'A vote of no confidence?' he hissed. 'What in . . . The hell with them! They can't do this to me!'

'They just *did*, Whiteley. An' you're *still* sittin' in my chair.'

Whiteley stood up and leaned across the desk, his face suffused with blood. 'I signed a contract!' he blustered.

'Me too,' Sam replied mildly. 'The only difference is that yours was *cancelled*.'

'The hell you say! You put them up to this!'

Sam eyed him steadily. 'Maybe I did,' he allowed. 'I had you pegged for a wrong 'un the minute I first clapped eyes on you. But I didn't know the half of it till I spoke to Coulson an' Marvin an' the rest of the town council last night.' He moved a step nearer the desk, as if claiming the area as his own. 'There's nothin' worse than a crooked lawman, Whiteley. An' from all I've heard, it seems you're a mite too friendly with this here Stover clan to be trusted with a badge.'

Whiteley's lantern jaw firmed up. 'The Stovers?' he echoed. 'Just what is *that* supposed to mean?'

Sam eyed him bleakly. 'You take your pay from one side or the other,' he replied. 'But not from *both*. Understand me now? Good. Now get the hell out of my office — and then get the hell out of town.'

They traded stares for a long, tense moment. Then Whiteley reached behind him and grabbed up his jacket. As he shrugged into it, the anger on his face slowly eased into a smile. But there was nothing pleasant about the curling of his thick lips. Indeed, his expression was more of a sneer.

'You want my badge,' he said in a low, trembly voice, 'you can *have* it.' He tore his cheap tin shield from his right lapel and slammed it down on the desk-top, making Mitzi flinch. 'And good luck to you,' he rasped contemptuously. 'Because you're gonna need it, believe me.'

Sam felt an unpleasant tingle wash through him, but kept his tone light. 'Oh? Why's that?'

Whiteley came around the desk and grabbed his beaver hat. 'You mean to say I know something you *don't*.'

'Just say what's on your mind an' go.'

'All right.' Whiteley chuckled without humor. 'You just inherited one heck of a problem, Judge. I hope for your sake that you can clear it up to everyone's satisfaction.'

'What's the problem?' Sam asked quietly.

'There was a murder last night,' Whiteley said, reaching for the door handle. 'Somebody up and killed Randolph Stover. Damn' near blew his head right off his shoulders.'

* * *

Whiteley slammed the door behind him, leaving Sam to eye his young companion through the haze of steam rising from his mug.

'Well I'll be damned,' Matt said, going over to one of the windows in order to watch the former deputy stalk away. 'He sure wasn't kiddin' when he said we'd just come into one heck of a problem, was he?'

He turned to Sam and watched him set down his mug and pick up the shield. The older man looked at the badge for a moment, then pinned it on. 'Nope,' he sighed. 'He sure wasn't.'

He fell silent for a while, watching Mitzi sniff her way around their new home. At last he reached a decision. 'All right, Matt. The job starts *here*. First, I want you to — '

Before he could go any further, the door burst open and a shortish man in a much-repaired black suit came racing in. He was in his early forties, with a round face, watery blue eyes and an impressive dark-gray handlebar moustache.

'Marshal! Marshal!' He pulled up suddenly, peering around the room in a blue funk. 'Where's the marshal?' he demanded.

Sam hooked a thumb at the shield on his chest. 'Right here,' he said. 'The name's Judge, just got started this mornin'. What's the trouble?'

The newcomer jabbed a muddy finger back the way he'd come. 'You gotta come quick!' he said in a high, desperate voice. 'They figger they've found 'im! Say they're gonna string 'im up!'

Sam stepped closer, narrowing his eyes. 'Who?' he snapped. 'Who have they found?'

The shortish man looked up into his face. 'Why, the killer, o' course! The fellow who murdered Randolph Stover!'

* * *

'For God's sake, untie me! I didn't have anything to do with it, I tell you!'

Jess Coltrain's transparent blue eyes flared as he backhanded his prisoner across the face. He grinned as the man lost balance and stumbled to his knees, spitting blood from a busted lip. 'Don't give us any of that, Harrigan! We heard you threaten Mr Stover with our own ears!' He reached down, grabbed the bewhiskered little miner by the shoulder of his broadcloth jacket and yanked him erect. 'Said he'd pay for roughin' you up, you did! An' by God, you *made* him pay!'

He shoved the smaller man up the grassy slope, away from the chuckling creek, and watched him stumble and stagger reluctantly toward Coltrain's partner, Johnny Baker. Baker, holding their horses about a dozen feet away, kept his hooded gaze on Harrigan's comrades. One of them had lit out shortly after they'd arrived, most probably to try and find Dick Whiteley, but the rest of the placer miners just stood there along the creek's slippery brown banks, their quest for gold temporarily forgotten, their faces still showing shock at the suddenness of events.

It was no secret that Pat Harrigan was one of Randolph Stover's most vocal opponents. Not one of them had ever relished paying the dead man's inflated prices, but in King Creek there was no choice. Harrigan, however, had always taken Stover's profiteering personally.

Still, he wasn't a murderer. Leastways, they didn't *think* so.

Coltrain and Baker, though, they had other ideas.

They had ridden out to Harrigan's modest claim just fifteen minutes earlier. At once tension had filled the pleasantly-cool early-morning air. One by one, Harrigan's fellow miners had stopped work to watch events unfold.

Within minutes the whole story had come out. They'd already heard that Randolph had been shot dead, of course. That kind of news always travelled fast. But that Harrigan was being considered as the chief suspect came as a total surprise.

Now the placer miners watched

Coltrain shove Harrigan further up the slope. First there would be an audience with Kate Stover. She would likely curse him, attempt to have a confession beaten out of him. But whether Harrigan was guilty or not, the outcome would be the same — death by hanging.

There wasn't a man there who didn't want to stop the matter before it got out of hand. Justice was one thing, but a lynching . . .

Then again, who among them had balls enough to go up against a Stover man? Besides which, evidence *was* evidence — they guessed.

That Harrigan despised Randolph Stover was well-known. That he had threatened Stover with some unspecified form of revenge yesterday morning he had not even bothered to deny. The single most damning fact, however, was that Harrigan could not account satisfactorily for his movements between a quarter of eight and eight-thirty the previous night, which was widely reckoned to be the time during which Randolph had been murdered. According to Harrigan, he'd bedded down early. He'd been feeling sore from the beating Baker and Coltrain had given him that morning, and in no mood for his customary evening trip into town.

Still, a lynching . . .

One of the miners, a sober-looking man with a black goatee beard and the manner of a preacher, finally broke the spell. Stalking up the slope with the wide shovel still clasped in his hands, he put himself on a course that would intercept the men who intended to hang Harrigan. He wore black pants and thick red braces over a grubby, wrinkled shirt. His name was Naylor, and he was of an age with Harrigan — about forty.

When no more than twenty feet separated them, he raised his voice. He had a deep voice that would have sounded good coming from a pulpit.

'Hi, you, Coltrain! Just hold up a minute!'

Harrigan came to a halt and twisted around. The small miner looked even more disheveled than usual. His thin, ruddy face appeared twice as haggard, and his blue eyes were lackluster and hopeless. The sweat of fear had plastered his thinning, dust-colored hair across his forehead, and already his lower lip was starting to swell.

A second later, Coltrain had also fixed the newcomer with a fiery glare, but as he watched Naylor come closer, the look on his long, sharp face was one of irritation rather than anger. 'Watch yourself, Naylor,' he warned. 'This is none of your beeswax. Back off now an' we'll say no more about it.'

But backing off was not something Naylor was prepared to do, not now that he'd overcome his apprehension and actually taken that first step.

'I'll not interfere with the workings of the law,' he replied in his clear, booming voice. 'But what you two are planning has nothing to do with justice.'

Coltrain set himself directly in front of the miner, his legs spread for balance and his fists bunched for effect. The tanned face beneath the shadow of his smoke-gray hat-brim was carved from granite. 'You finished?' he asked sarcastically.

Expression grim, Naylor shook his head. In another place and at another time, he might have been a Biblical prophet. 'No, I have not,' he replied. 'Look, man; maybe Harrigan *is* guilty, as you say. But what if he *isn't*? That decision's not yours to make! The man should get a proper trial — '

Coltrain began to turn away, dismissing him with the gesture. Naylor, growing increasingly fearful for Harrigan, reached out and set one calloused paw on his right forearm, to make him pause. 'If you won't listen to me,' he implored, 'at least listen to your conscience!'

Coltrain spun back fast, and back-handed him savagely. For just an instant, his wolfish face took on a rabid snarl. Then Naylor hit the ground on his back, the shovel falling from his grip. His eyes were glazed and blood oozed from one nostril like a fat red slug.

'I haven't *got* a conscience,' Coltrain told him in a low, dangerous voice. 'You just remember that next time you figger to lay a hand on me.'

Naylor squinted up at him with his jaw muscles clenching.

'Next time,' Coltrain hissed, 'I'll kill you.'

Growing aware of the dark muttering that swept through the rest of the miners, Coltrain suddenly shifted his attention from the fallen man. Addressing all of them, he said, 'This is Stover business, you hear me? A Stover's been killed, an' we're here to make sure his killer pays for it!' He glanced at Baker, then indicated Harrigan, who was standing between them with his sorrowful gaze fixed on Naylor. 'Get him mounted up,' Coltrain barked. Softly he added,

'Then let's get the hell out of here.'

Baker had just taken a pace towards Harrigan, intending to push him across to the spare saddle-horse they'd brought along with them, when one of the watching miners, attracted by something happening off to the south, turned away from them. As the sound of hoof beats started to grow in volume, so more miners began to switch their gaze.

Coltrain, Baker, their hapless prisoner and the man called Naylor soon joined them, squinting in order to make out the identities of the three riders approaching from the direction of town.

'That's Murdock!' one of the miners muttered, recognizing their short, mustached comrade, who had lit out earlier to go fetch the marshal.

'Can't discern who he's got with 'im,' said another man.

'Me neither.'

Baker, however, whose eyesight was passably keen, had no trouble in recognizing Murdock's companions, and wasted no time in passing the news on to Coltrain. 'Hey, Jess . . . that's the old geezer as pulled iron on us yest'day mornin', an' the kid who gave you that puffy jaw.'

Coltrain could identify them for himself now. Again he planted himself firmly up there on that slope of patchy grass and dirt, left hand rubbing the bruise Matt had given him the day before, right hand keeping close company with the walnut grips of his .45.

4

When the riders were no more than ten feet away they reined in, bringing their horses to a stiff-legged halt that tore clods of earth out of the ground. Murdock, having done his bit, edged his ribby piebald a little to one side, then allowed it to carry him out of the firing line.

Coltrain glanced from the older man to the younger. 'Well, fan my brow,' he said, grinning insolently. 'Look what we got here, John.' To Sam he said, 'You always make a habit of buyin' in to other folks' business, mister?'

'Only when it's agin the law,' Sam replied easily. Using his left hand, he gestured to Harrigan. 'An' I hear you mean to do this feller some serious harm.'

'He's a killer,' Coltrain said as if that explained everything. 'He killed Randolph Stover, nothin' surer.'

'That's for the law to decide.'

'Hell, you yourself heard him threaten Stover yesterday mornin'!'

Sam nodded. 'Sure. But all that'll come out at the trial.'

Coltrain frowned, not quite sure where Sam fitted into all this. 'Just who *are* you?' he asked bluntly.

Sam indicated the shield. 'The new marshal.'

Baker shifted uncomfortably, only now noticing the badge. 'The new — ! What happened to Whiteley?'

Sam's smile was cool. '*Me*,' he answered, dismounting. 'Now, step aside from yonder prisoner, you two. Harrigan; I'm takin' you in as much for your own protection as anythin' else. Until a better candidate comes along, I got to consider you a prime suspect in this business.'

Harrigan nodded, still looking pale. 'Uh, sure. But I'll tell you what I just told these two. I didn't have nothin' to do with it, marshal. By Godfrey, I don't even own a pistol!'

'Tell it to the jury,' Sam told him, moving closer.

Up in the saddle, Matt tensed as Baker and Coltrain, far from stepping aside, actually came nearer, to stand between Sam and his prisoner. For a second the young man's right hand slipped down to one of his matched Tranters. Then he hesitated. If he knew Sam, then the new marshal of King Creek would prefer to settle this without gunplay. For one thing, there were too many innocent bystanders strung out along the creek-banks. For another, this might be a good opportunity to prove his mettle to the Stover men in another, less permanent, way.

Forcing himself to sit tight, Matt waited to see what Sam would do next.

The veteran town-tamer pulled up maybe two feet from Baker and Coltrain. The expression on his seamed visage was one of disdain. Shaking his head, he said, 'Mayhaps you boys didn't hear me. I told you to step *aside* from the prisoner.' His eyes went flat. '*Do it*,' he advised with quiet authority. 'Or suffer the consequence.'

Baker's round face split into a grin that flared the nostrils of his hooked nose. His tone was mocking when he said, 'Well, I'll give you credit for one thing, marshal — you sure talk big for a dusty old fart with one foot in the grave.'

Much to his surprise, Sam smiled too. 'Why, thanks,' he said politely.

Then he kicked Baker right in the sphericals.

Even as the shorter of the two bully-boys fell away from him, singing top C as he clutched his stinging manhood, Sam was launching a left hook at Coltrain's jaw. He wasn't as fast as he used to be. Felt like he was trying to fight under water, in fact. But he was still pretty sudden. He caught Coltrain dead on and felt the blow connect all the way up to his shoulder.

With Coltrain off balance, he quickly stepped in and followed up with a right jab. Coltrain yelped as the punch jarred his already puffy jaw, then slipped on the slick grass and fell hard onto his rump.

Sam shook his hands to restore some feeling. 'Now,' he began, throwing a glance across at Baker, who was on his hands and knees ten feet away, spewing up his breakfast.

Before he could go on, however, Coltrain powered back to his feet and clawed at his short-barreled Colt.

Matt yelled, '*Sam!*'

But Sam didn't need any warning. Already all too aware of the innocent men lining the muddy banks, he wanted to avoid shooting at all costs. He moved in quickly, crowding Coltrain before he could start blasting, grabbed his right wrist in a vice-like grip and squeezed tight, until he felt the bones grind.

Coltrain cried out again through clenched teeth. His transparent blue eyes burned into Sam's long, slightly mournful face. Then, at last, his fingers straightened out and his handgun fell to the ground.

'*Sonofabitch!*' Coltrain spat, furious. '*Bastard!*'

He pushed Sam away and staggered back a few feet, smudges of high color in his hollow cheeks. He was still swearing when he reached behind him and brought out an unsociable-looking Confederate ten-inch Bowie knife.

'*I'll kill you now, old man!*' he hissed.

He came in fast, mad as hell, and the Confederate Bowie chopped at the air in front of Sam. For one split second Sam considered hauling iron and plugging him where he stood. But then, as Sam backed off from him, he stumbled on the wide-bladed shovel that Naylor had dropped when Coltrain had struck him.

A little further up the slope, Baker made to rise and join in the fray. Matt quickly slipped from his saddle and kicked the fellow's legs out from under him. 'Just stay put, partner,' he said, drawing one of his handguns and jabbing the long barrel against the soft flesh just beneath Baker's right ear. 'You're *out* of it.'

Sam, meanwhile, bent to scoop up the shovel just as Coltrain, bellowing his rage, came charging forward with the knife extended to arm's length.

Quickly Sam got a hold on the shovel, brought it around and slammed it against Coltrain's knifehand. At once Coltrain released his grip on the weapon and screamed like a woman. Before he could recover, Sam decided to finish it fast, and in the only way that a man like Coltrain would understand — with violence.

Wielding the shovel not unlike a baseball bat, he stepped to one side and slammed the flat of the blade right into Coltrain's exposed midriff.

The Stover man's breath fairly flew out of him as he staggered backwards. While he was still blundering all over the slope, Sam struck him again. The metal blade practically sang as it dented his ribs. Coltrain fell over, rolled a couple of feet, then came to rest on his back.

Within seconds Sam had appeared above him. Now he held the shovel *like* a shovel, as though ready to start digging. The edge of the wide, dirty blade felt cold against Coltrain's bare throat.

'Had enough yet?' Sam snapped, scalding him with a hot gaze.

Coltrain opened his mouth to reply, then went very pale. His eyes rolled up into his head and he swooned like a Southern belle.

Pausing just long enough to make sure the blond hard case was still breathing, Sam straightened up and tossed the shovel away. Down by the creek twenty or thirty feet away, the placer miners watched him in silence. Breathing hard from his exertions, he turned around and picked up Coltrain's .45. Matt had already relieved Baker of his Merwin & Hulbert .44, and reaching out, Sam took hold of that, too.

Going back down to the water, he

eyed the miners sidelong. They still didn't know for sure what to make of him. They'd probably grown used to having a crooked sonofabitch like Dick Whiteley running things, so the shield on his chest counted for little.

It was time to change all that.

Sam looked down at the hard cases' guns, then turned his mild gray eyes onto the men standing along both sides of the creek.

'You been findin' gold an' silver down there,' he said, nodding to the sluggish current. He threw the guns into the water, enjoying the cool splash they made. 'Reckon you'll find some lead an' iron as well, after this.'

A little way down the bank, a fresh-faced miner showed his teeth in a smile. Another one chuckled, more out of relief than anything else.

Sam went back up the slope to where Baker sat pale-faced, with a few puke-stains on his shirtfront. Sam eyed him sternly. 'You listen up real good now, Baker. The law's gonna find

Stover's killer, you hear me? An' when it finds him, it's gonna punish him. Got that?'

Baker nodded, looking up at him from under lowered eyebrows.

'Good. Now get your buddy up an' out of here. An' remember — if any o' these men run into any more trouble, it's *you* I'll come lookin' for.'

When he was sure he'd impressed his sincerity on the hard case, the new marshal turned to his prisoner. 'Harrigan, I'm placin' you in the custody of my deputy, here. You behave yourself an' we'll get along fine.'

It was Harrigan's turn to nod. 'You'll get no trouble from me. I got nothin' to hide.'

'Right. Matt — I want you to get on back to the office. Go through the files an' find out who handles all the coroner's duties for these parts, then go chase 'im up an' see what he's got to say about the murder. Oh, an' while you're about it, have a word with all the local sawbones, see if our friend with the arm full of buckshot got himself patched up after all.'

'Yo.'

'An' don't let this jasper out of your sight,' Sam added, pointing at Harrigan. 'Was this a normal state of affairs, I'd suggest you lock him up in the jail, but there's no tellin' what'd become of him if he was left unattended, so he'd best go along with you.'

Matt inclined his head. 'Right. But what'll *you* be doin' while I'm chasin' all over town?'

Sam smiled unpleasantly. 'I'll be takin' a little trek up to Crane Rock,' he replied. 'Figger it's about time I paid my respects to the rest o' them Stovers.'

* * *

Crane Rock rose green and gray over the town. The Stover house sat halfway up its gentle, north-facing slope, among white brittlebrush, speckle-pod loco and the odd claret-cup hedgehog cactus. Everyone knew where to find it, and once Sam got directions, even he had to admit that it was kind of hard to miss.

But as he allowed his old strawberry roan to pick its way up the dusty incline, he saw that the house, while grand, was just another prefabricated structure shipped out from back East. It stood two storeys in height, and its walls were of one-inch planed pine. Six cement steps led up to a neatly-fenced veranda. Two ornate wooden columns flanked a surprisingly plain front door. The roof was shingled, and peaked with an impressive turret. The windows, each curtained with bone-white lace, watched his approach through milky eyes.

A man lounged in a chair on the veranda, just left of the front door. He was thirty, short, with a wide, prize-fighter's face and oily black hair. He wore a gray shirt, black pants and a brown leather gunbelt holding a Smith & Wesson Russian. On his lap lay a

Winchester. He stood up as Sam reined in and cooled his saddle. Sam saw that he was only about five and a half feet tall, but solid through the chest and arms. He had the kind of eyes that life had soured. They were black and belligerent.

'Help you?' he asked as Sam tied his reins around one of the veranda posts.

'Hope so. The name's Judge. I'm the new town m — '

'I know all that.'

Sam raised one eyebrow. News sure travelled fast around here. 'Like to see Mrs. Stover, if she's at home,' he went on. 'Understand there's been some trouble in the family.' Cautiously he began to climb the cement steps.

Immediately the other man stepped into his path. 'Uh-huh. No visitors. Mrs. Stover's in mournin'.'

'I can understand that. Didn't expect to find her anyway else. But the way I hear it, one of her boys was murdered last night. Like to ask her an' her survivin' kin a few questions before the trail gets too cold.'

The hired hand's voice grew chilly. 'I *said* no visitors.' He turned sideways on, so that he could cover Sam with the Winchester he held at waist-height. 'What's the matter with you, old man? You hard of hearin'?'

Sam's sigh spoke volumes. Seemed like nobody respected his elders anymore. He said, 'I'd take it kindly if you'd point that there long-gun someplace else.'

The hard case grinned. 'Would you, now?'

Sam nodded. 'Well, let me put it this way; you either point it someplace else of your own free will, or I'll come up there and do it for you.'

The hard case snorted, clearly amused by the older man's words. 'I'd like to see you try,' he said.

'All right,' Sam said tiredly. But what happened next was so swift that he never got to see it at all.

Sam reached out, grabbed the rifle by the barrel, jerked it out of the startled hard case's hands and slammed it back into his face.

The hard case hit the veranda boards in a heap.

Glancing around to make sure he hadn't been seen, Sam propped the rifle against the nearest of the columns flanking the door, bent, took the limp figure under the arms and hauled him upright. Depositing him back in his chair, Sam examined his face. He'd have a nasty bruise for sure — damn' thing was coming up already — and his nose might smart for a couple of days, but otherwise he was just unconscious.

Arranging the figure as best he could, he ejected all the shells from the long-gun, then placed it back across his lap. A moment later he jangled the bell-pull and cleared his throat expectantly.

The door opened almost at once. Chances were that someone inside had heard the hard case falling down and been on their way to make sure he was all right.

The someone was Dick Whiteley.

His surprise was obvious. Sam Judge was clearly the last person he'd expected to see. Within moments, however, he'd recovered sufficiently to step forward, effectively blocking off Sam's view of the gloomy hallway beyond.

'What the hell are you doing up here?' Whiteley demanded. Before Sam could reply, he glanced down at the hard case sitting in the chair with the rifle across his lap and frowned. 'Faver . . . ?'

'Shh,' Sam said pleasantly. 'He's asleep.'

'Asl — Just what do you think — ?'

'I'm here to see Kate Stover, Whiteley, so either get back inside there an' announce me, or get out of my way.'

'Now see here — '

'It's all right, Mr Whiteley. I'll see Marshal Judge in the parlor.'

The voice was like cool running water. It made Whiteley freeze, then turn slowly to face the woman who owned it. As he moved to one side, Sam got his first look at Kate Stover.

She was a very well-preserved fifty-year-old, garbed entirely in black. She had a small, evenly-proportioned face crowned by a spill of ash-blonde curls, worn high. Her eyes were chocolate-brown and bright, the way Randolph's had been. Her nose was small and direct, her pale pink lips heart-shaped and kissable. She stood maybe five feet four, and her still-neat frame was encased in a tailored black dress that flared out from her trim waist. Only her face and hands were visible there in the gloom, as she mirrored Sam's blunt appraisal. Then she turned with a silky rustle and seemed to glide back down the hallway and into what was, presumably, the parlor.

Whiteley watched her go with something very much like devotion on his face. Then he turned back to Sam and got all scowly again. 'You'd better go in,' he said quietly. 'Mrs Stover don't like to be kept waiting.'

Sam stepped past him into a reasonably spacious hallway. A heavy wooden sideboard ran the length of one wall. In the opposite corner stood a yellow-faced grandfather clock. His boots made a lot of noise on the polished floorboards as he went through the doorway and into the parlor.

The first things he noticed were the flowers. Hell, he couldn't be *off* of noticing them. Whole bunches of carnations, wild roses and irises occupied vases and bowls all over the place; on the mantelpiece, on the harmonium, on the neat little chest of drawers and on the shelves in the alcoves to either side of the cold hearth. Apart from all the flowers, the room appeared quite ordinary. Real back-East wallpaper had been tacked up over the pine walls, he noticed.

'Now, Marshal Judge,' said the woman sitting on the horsehair sofa beside the harmonium. 'How may I help you?'

He saw her better in this light, and had his initial impression of strength, determination and near-classical good-looks confirmed. He took off his Stetson and ran a hand through his thinning gray-black hair. 'My condolences on the loss of your son, ma'am,' he said politely. 'I'm sorry to intrude like this. I guess you must be takin' it pretty bad.'

She turned her shiny brown eyes on him, and he saw that they were sore around the rims. 'Have you ever lost a son?' she enquired.

'No, ma'am,' he replied. '*Found* one, but never lost one.'

'No-one can express the sense of . . . devastation that loss brings with it.'

'I can imagine.'

'You are here about Randolph, I presume?'

He nodded. 'Yes'm. That an' one or two other matters.'

'Such as?'

Sam heard footsteps descending the hallway staircase. A moment later the parlor door swung open and two men came clattering in. Their gaze moved from the woman on the sofa to Sam, standing over by the mantel with his hat in his hands. They sized him up quickly, and did not seem impressed by what they saw. Sam could hardly say that he blamed them.

The eldest of the two men was about thirty. He stood tall, slim and elegant in his black Prince Albert and paper-white shirt. He had a long, tanned face with brown eyes, prominent cheekbones, a straight, sharp nose and thin, lemony lips. His hair was thick and brown, but so heavily macassared that it appeared black. He wore gold rings on most of his fingers.

His companion was no more than twenty or so. He was three inches shorter than the fellow alongside him, and not quite so brawny. He had a thin, pale face, sick brown eyes and short hair the color of butter. Unless Sam missed his guess, the youngster was ailing with something, maybe consumption. He wore jeans, a sky-blue shirt and a thick black armband.

'Who're you?' the elder of the two newcomers asked without preamble.

Sam told them. 'An' I guess you'll be Mrs. Stover's other boys, Dale an' Gene.'

Kate Stover came up off the sofa and moved soundlessly across to them. 'Yes,' she said, placing one hand on Dale's black sleeve. 'These are my *other* sons.'

It was Sam's turn to do a little sizing up. So here was the elegant Dale, who ran the *Pot of Gold*, and young Gene, who handled things down at the Stover's freight operation.

'I asked you a question,' Dale said bluntly. 'What are you doing here, disturbing my mother when she's — '

'I'm makin' enquiries into your brother's death,' Sam cut in. 'So's I can find the sonofabitch who killed him.'

'We *know* who killed him,' Gene said, stepping forward. He had a harsh,

bubbly voice, and carried a handkerchief at the ready in his left hand.

It was consumption for sure, then.

'Who?' Sam asked. 'Pat Harrigan?'

He saw surprise on all their faces for
an instant, until they closed up. Then
Dale said, 'Why not? Jess Coltrain tells
me you yourself was a witness when he
threatened Randy yesterday morning.'

'I was,' Sam replied evenly. 'But
threatenin' a man's one thing; takin' the
law into your own hands is somethin'
else.'

'Marshal Judge,' Kate Stover said in a
voice like Alaska. 'Being new to these
climes, maybe there are one or two
facts I should draw to your attention.'

Sam matched her tone. 'Maybe there
are.'

'To begin with, that shield you're
wearing counts for nothing around
here. *Nothing*. The only law in King
Creek is Stover's Law. You might find it
to your advantage to remember that.'

'Well, I'll try.'

'Now,' she said, trying to ignore his

110

insufferable self-confidence. 'My eldest son has been murdered, and I want the miscreant responsible to pay for it. I'm not interested in the workings of the law. All I want, all *any* of us wants, is revenge, pure and simple. Do I make myself clear?'

'As glass,' Sam replied. 'An' for your information, I've already arrested Harrigan.'

He saw more surprise on their faces.

'Furthermore,' he went on, 'if I can't find a better suspect, I'll see to it that he stands trial. But I think we'd all better get one thing straight. I've heard some pretty unsavory tales about you Stovers, so I'm tellin' you now — you toe the line an' stop all these shenanigans of yours, or you'll answer for it.'

'I don't believe you quite understood what I just said, Marshal — '

'Oh, I understood good enough, Mrs. Stover. But no matter what you might say to the contrary, ma'am, *I'm* the law here now. Not you, not some poor s.o.b. you shot half to death, an' not a puppet who can be bought off like Dick Whiteley.' Sam glared at each of them in turn. 'I catch any of you breakin' the rules,' he warned grimly, 'I'm gonna throw you in jail.'

Outside, the grandfather clock began to toll the hour.

'Sounds to me,' said Dale, 'like you're declaring war.'

Sam nodded sharply. 'It should,' he replied. ''Cause *I am*.'

* * *

By the time he got back to the law office, Harrigan had been locked in the communal cell and Matt was going through the contents of the wooden file-cabinet.

'Have any luck?' Sam asked, hanging his hat on the peg in the door and going over to the coffee-pot.

Matt rolled the file-cabinet drawer shut. 'Local sawbones by the name of Newton's been handlin' all the coroner's duties for King Creek these last couple months,' he reported. 'Went to see him, like you said.'

'And?'

'An' apart from tellin' me that Stover's face was caved in by a heavy-caliber shell that killed him outright, he couldn't shed much light,' Matt said. 'He *did* point me in the direction of two other doctors, though, an' I checked in with both.' He paused. 'Sawbones named Kramer patched up a feller with an arm full of buckshot yesterday afternoon.'

'You get a description?'

'Sure. Tall feller, dark hair, dark eyes, thick lips, hooked beak. Could have some Indian blood. Kramer says he's seen him around town before, but didn't know his name, or where to find him.'

Sam tasted the black, stewed coffee. It was hot as Hades. 'Well, it's somethin', at least.'

'How'd you fare?'

Sam told him.

'So you've thrown down the gauntlet,' Matt said with a grim smile.

'Yep.' Sam took another careful sip. 'What happens next is up to them.'

'Marshal?' It was Harrigan.

Sam threw him a glance as he flopped into the Douglas chair behind the desk. 'Yeah?'

The whiskery little Irishman was pressed close to the bars of the cell. 'You get any notions from them Stovers as to who *really* killed Randolph?' he asked.

Sam smiled. 'Not really. They seem pretty certain it was *you*.'

'But I'm innocent, I tell you! Sweet Jesus, I don't even own a gun!'

'All right, all right, pipe down for the love'a Mike!' Sam set his mug aside. 'Still, from what I hear of him, you could pick any man-jack in this town and he'd have a reason to want this here Randolph dead — you included. But for what it's worth, I don't see you as a killer, Harrigan.'

'Well, thank the Lord for that.'

Still, Sam thought, *someone'd* plugged the sonofabitch — and he guessed he'd be well advised to find whoever it was quick.

'Oh, yeah,' said Matt.

He looked up. 'What?'

'Remember Sullivan, the assayer, from last night?'

Sam cast his mind back to their meeting with the unofficial town council out at Pearl's place the previous evening. His memory showed him the image of a stooped young fellow with a sweeping red moustache and blue eyes. 'Feller with the freckles an' spectacles?' he asked.

'That's him,' Matt nodded. 'He came lookin' for you 'bout twenty minutes ago. Said he'd 'preciate a word whenever you get the chance.'

'He say what it was about?'

'Nope. Just that he'd like to see you as soon as possible.'

Sam mulled that over. The assayer had said little during the meeting, though he'd been among the first to support a vote of no confidence in Dick Whiteley. 'Think I'll take a turn around town an' pay him a visit, then,' the veteran lawman decided. 'But first . . . '

'Yeah?'

'First I figure to grab me a late breakfast.' Sam smiled with surprising good-humor. 'All this keepin' the peace has surely sharpened my appetite.'

5

Sam's turn around town took him back to East Street, where he stopped off at Pearl's place, just to make sure she and her old man were bearing up.

This morning Pearl had somehow managed to get Jack out of bed and into one of the fireside chairs. Away from the creased sheets and pillows, the former marshal of King Creek looked much better in the face, and clearer in the eyes. But the body beneath his collarless white shirt and denim pants was still pitifully wasted, and he was all too aware of the fact.

Sam accepted a cup of Arbuckle's finest and sat for a time just shooting the breeze. Both Pearl and Jack were keen to hear of all that had happened, and both expressed a desire that Sam should tread softly around the Stovers.

Just before he rose to leave, Sam

asked if Jack had any ideas as to who might have wanted Randolph dead bad enough to do something about it. Pearl's husband shook his head slowly. 'There's too many to list,' he replied frankly. 'Though I doubt that most of 'em would have the guts to pull the trigger, or even hire it done, for that matter.'

'That's about what I figured. You know Harrigan at all?'

'Just to pass the time of day. But he's always struck me as the type who keeps his nose clean.'

'That's how he strikes me, too. But no matter. I keep diggin' around, I'll come up with somethin' sooner or later.'

Sam grabbed his hat off the table and clapped it down on his head. At the door, one more thought occurred to him. 'Matt turned up a description of the feller we think you might've shot yest'day mornin'.' He repeated the details Matt had given him back at the office. 'Strike any chords?' he asked keenly.

Again Denton shook his head. 'No, dammit. But maybe he's kind of new to town, in which case I wouldn't've come across him before.' His voice dropped. 'Not cooped up here, like a cripple.'

Sam nodded, deciding not to comment on his sudden show of self-pity. 'Well, I'll be gettin' along. Thanks for the coffee, Pearl.'

'Hey, Judge.'

Sam paused in the doorway, then turned back to face Denton. 'Yeah?'

'That badge,' Denton said softly. 'Looks awful good on you. Think it'll become permanent?'

Sam shook his head. 'Hardly. I'm only fillin' in till you get back in harness.'

Denton's smile was sour. 'I don't believe you'll ever see that day dawn.'

'I'd better,' Sam said firmly. 'You got a wife to support, mister.'

Back on Main, Sam took pot-luck and entered the first canvas eatery he came to. The off-white tent was large and airless. Two long trestle tables with bench seats ran along either side of the central aisle. The place was doing pretty fair mid-morning business. For the most part, its patrons were tuckered-out miners who'd just finished early shifts below ground.

Sam strode down to the plank-and-barrel counter that separated the tables from the cooking-area. Almost at once he became aware of an ominous lowering of conversation among the other customers.

A blonde woman with premature age-lines stood behind the counter. Behind her a fat Mexican in a sweaty undershirt was frying bacon on a griddle. The girl asked him what he wanted and Sam told her — bacon, eggs and a small stack of pancakes.

'Here,' said a man behind Sam. 'I'll get that.'

Sam turned just as the speaker rose from his place at the end of the left-side trestle table and dug into his pants'-pocket for some change. He was a big fellow whose dusty, dirt-smudged face was almost hidden beneath a bushy black beard.

'Do I know you?' Sam asked as the man clapped a few coins down on the makeshift counter.

'No sir.'

'Well, if you'll pardon me askin', why're you so all-fired keen to buy me breakfast?'

The man frowned down at him from a lofty six feet six. He could have been any age from thirty to fifty. His hazel eyes were bright and humorous, his nose no more than a lumpy ball on his face, and his teeth were stained with chewing tobacco. He raised his right hand and tapped the shield pinned on Sam's jacket. 'You're the new marshal, ain'tcha?'

Sam nodded cautiously. 'Yeah.'

'An' you stood up to them two gunnies, Baker an' Coltrain, didn't you? To stop 'em from lynchin' Pat Harrigan?'

'Well . . . yeah.'

The big fellow grinned amiably.

'Well, don't ast such stupid questions, then. Any friend o' Harrigan's is a friend of ours, am I right, boys?'

The miners who had been watching the exchange suddenly voiced hearty agreement. Several of them even pushed along the benches to make room for Sam to join them.

'Make yourself at home, marshal,' said Sam's benefactor. 'You're in good comp'ny here.' He struck out one calloused palm. 'The name's Connors, by the way. Dave Connors.'

'Sam Judge,' said Sam, shaking with him. 'An' it does my heart real good to meet you-all, 'cause so far today you're about the only set of *hombres* I've clapped eyes on who didn't want to see my head on a pole!'

* * *

About an hour later Sam quit the eatery and promised to come back soon. As he swung left and headed for Walt Sullivan's independent assay office, he reflected on all the men Connors had introduced to him. He could hardly recall the names, but each of them had struck him as a possibly useful ally if and when the Stovers decided to call a showdown.

The time was approaching one o'clock and Main Street was as chaotic now as it had been when he and Matt had first ridden in the previous day. Dodging fellow pedestrians, Sam caught a glimpse of Randolph Stover's general store across the busy thorough-fare. A sign on the door read CLOSED UNTIL FURTHER NOTICE. A wide brown stain on the plank boardwalk just in front of the store that was all too recognizable as dried blood showed him where Stover had fallen and died. Part of the doorframe had been chewed away by the killer's bullet, as it exited the back of Randolph's head.

The motive for the crime had been revenge, he was sure. According to the information he'd been able to prise out of the dead man's uncooperative kin, the corpse hadn't been robbed, and neither had the store been broken into. Even Randolph's diamond stick pin had been left undisturbed in his sky-blue cravat.

It had to be revenge, then, he mused, taking out a cigar and biting off the end. Someone looking to get even over something. But what? And *who*?

He lit the cigar, tossed the match away and continued along Main until he reached the mud-splattered tent from which Walt Sullivan operated his assay business.

Sullivan himself had his back to the tent entrance. He was hunched over a narrow table on the other side of a makeshift counter similar to the one in use back at the eatery, hard at work performing what looked like a complicated test on the ore samples some hopeful sourdough had brought in for checking.

Sam eyed the place with interest, impressed by all the bowls, funnels, test-tubes and beakers on the low shelves Sullivan had set up, as well as the fat bottles filled with chemicals and the finely-balanced scales resting in the glass case to the young man's right.

Sam cleared his throat, just to let Sullivan know he was there, then took a pace or two deeper into the tent.

Sullivan turned around, holding a small, chemical-filled dropper in one hand and a thin glass tube in the other. He was a young man, maybe twenty-eight or thirty, with round shoulders, a bookworm's stoop and a pleasant, freckle-splashed face. He peered at Sam through small, round glasses, with the mouth beneath his sweeping red moustache forming an anticipatory O. When he recognized Sam he set his tools aside, wiped his hands on the front of his dark-blue overalls and reached out to shake.

'Marshal Judge! The very man!' He had a light, back-East accent, maybe Boston, Sam thought. There in the vaguely yellow light of the breeze-swept tent, with his narrow-brimmed hat shoved back on his short, wiry red hair and a stiff, white wing collar poking up from beneath an old woolen sweater the color of cow-crap, he looked not unlike a college professor. 'It's good of you to call. I imagine you've been pretty busy with all this hooraw about Randolph Stover.'

'Forget it.'

'Well, come on through, man, and have a seat.'

It was actually a stool with three long legs, onto which Sam set his weight gently. 'I see that you've arrested a fellow for the murder,' Sullivan said.

'On *suspicion* of murder.'

'Oh, yes. Quite.'

'Matt tells me you called by the office earlier on,' Sam said, puffing smoke into the air.

'Yes, I did. After all the talk last night, I got to thinking, and came up with an idea I'd appreciate your views on.'

'Sure, go ahead.'

'Well, basically, I believe King Creek

126

offers all manner of opportunities for a fellow with foresight, marshal. And I also believe the time has come for me to branch out . . . speculate, if you will.'

Sam pulled his cigar from his mouth and inspected the glowing amber tip. 'Go on.'

'What I'm proposing will, I hope, benefit both myself and the good citizens of this town. Because, in short, I intend to set up as a rival to the late Randolph Stover, selling everything from needles to bootlaces — but without the hefty mark-up, of course. I've already had a word with Bryce Colbourne, who's putting up that block of wood-built stores just along the way, so premises are no problem. Neither is staff; I've been sounding out one or two potential candidates just this morning, in fact.'

'So what do you need *me* for?'

Sullivan's normally cheerful face darkened. 'Well, I daresay you've heard about what happens to people who have the temerity to set up in competition to the Stovers. That's why I'll only go ahead with my plans if you can give me some assurance that I won't end up like all the rest.'

Sam snorted. 'Hell, to make good on a promise like that I'd have to ride shotgun on you twenty-four hours a day.'

'Well, maybe I haven't phrased the thing exactly as I mean it.' Sullivan paused. 'What I'm trying to say is, can I rely on you to tell these Stovers straight — that they had better hope nothing untoward happens to me or my business, because if it does, you'll know exactly who is responsible, and see to it that they pay the penalty?'

Sam considered that. It seemed a small price to pay to encourage a little honest trading in King Creek. 'I'll do it, sure,' he replied. 'But it's only fair to tell you that the Stovers've already shown scant regard for this here shield today. I couldn't guarantee that any-thin' I said would carry enough weight to make 'em lay off you.'

Sullivan nodded. 'Of course. But I don't expect miracles, marshal, just a little practical support from the law.'

'In that case, you've got it.'

'Capital, capital!' Sullivan enthused, taking Sam's hand and pumping it again. 'I believe I'll go ahead with my plans, then.'

'I wish you luck.'

'There's, ah, just one other thing.'

Sam chewed his cigar over to the corner of his mouth. 'I had an idea there might be.'

'It's a small matter, really, but of no little importance.'

'Spill it.'

'Very well. In order to stock my store, I'm going to have to send a couple of independent freighters out to the nearest supplier, in Dalhart. If the Stovers should get wind of what I'm up to, I doubt very seriously that they would ever reach their destination.'

Sam agreed that he had a point. 'You want an edge, then, is that it?' he asked.

'A little extra security?'

Sullivan nodded. 'Indeed, I was thinking that perhaps you could spare your deputy to, ah, 'ride shotgun' on my wagons.'

Again Sam turned the assayer's proposition over in his mind. He wasn't sure he could really spare Matt, but at the same time he'd feel a sight easier if his boy was out of town for a while. Furthermore, if Harrigan went along for the ride, it would relieve Sam of one more problem. 'I'll have a word with him an' see what we can work out,' he said at last.

'I'd be willing to pay you for your trouble, of course.'

'O' course,' said Sam. 'An' you will — to the tune of six months' free credit for Pearl an' Jack Denton.'

'*What?*'

'You heard. I doubt the town council's payin' Jack much more'n a pittance while he's laid up, so they could sure use some help makin' ends meet.'

It was Sullivan's turn to consider. 'If we can agree on *four* months' credit, we've got a deal.'

Sam rose from the stool. 'Right. I'll be movin' along, then, but either me or Matt'll stop by later this afternoon, once we've sorted everythin' out.'

'Of course. Thank you, marshal.'

'Oh, one other thing. It's just a chance, but you bein' in the minin' trade, maybe you've come across a feller could be connected to the blastin' business. He's tall, dark-haired, dark eyes, hooked nose. Might have some Indian blood.'

Sullivan nodded. 'He has. If he's the fellow I'm thinking of, he's half-Chippewa. Name of Coyote, I believe. Charlie Coyote.'

Sam eyed him keenly. 'Well thanks, Sullivan. You got no idea of his whereabouts, I suppose?'

Sullivan laughed. 'My dear marshal, I can go one better than that. The fellow walked right past this tent no more than five minutes ago!'

Sam hustled out onto the low board-walk and looked both ways along the busy street. Heavy wagons rumbled and clattered by, raising dust in both directions. Horseback riders and pedestrians only added to the confusion, and the sidewalks seemed just as bad, full of blocky miners and soiled doves out shopping.

'Damn . . . '

Sullivan joined him outside, adding his own myopic scrutiny to the search. 'There he is!' he said a moment later. 'Do you see him? About forty yards along, just crossing the street?'

Sam shook his head impatiently. 'Where?'

'*There*.'

'What's he wearin'?'

Sullivan squinted. 'A brown wool coat, blue denim pants and a gray hat. Do you see him *now*. Good heavens, marshal, you can't *miss* him. It looks as if he's hurt his left arm, because he's carrying it in a sling.'

For Sam, that clinched it. Coincidence was one thing, but this was something else again. Charlie Coyote was almost certainly the would-be murderer Jack Denton had peppered yesterday morning.

At last Sam spotted his target. He said, 'Thanks, Sullivan,' then broke into a trot, after the wounded man the young assayer had pointed out.

Charlie Coyote stepped up onto the opposite boardwalk and kept going. Although he kept looking around him, he maintained a steady pace. He didn't know he'd been rumbled yet, then.

When Sam was no more than sixty feet behind him, he slowed down. It was too crowded to brace him here in the street. Better if he followed the half-breed until they reached someplace a tad less busy.

Coyote was in his mid-thirties. The King Creek coroner had described him well. He had shoulder-length blue-black hair, a coppery skin just dark enough to hint at Indian parentage, shifty, restless black eyes and a hooked nose drooping down over thick, humorless lips. He was about six feet tall and built kind of stocky for a half-Chippewa. His left arm hung in a sling tied around his neck.

Sam saw that he wore a pistol in a cracked leather holster on his right hip.

They passed a barbershop and moved on. Coyote crossed a congested intersection and continued walking south. A photographer had set up his canvas studio midway along this block. Sam glanced through the open flap into the area out back and saw two miners gussied-up in their Sunday best, posing stiffly before a wood-and-brass camera. The miner who was seated held a pure white dove in his right hand.

Sam continued up the street, gaining just a little on his quarry. Then Coyote turned right, into a little cabin with the sign APOTHECARY hanging over the door. Sam began to trot again, to catch him up. A moment later he stepped into the drugstore's sweet-smelling interior.

Charlie Coyote was the only customer. He was standing by the big iron till, talking to the bald-headed proprietor in a low voice. As Sam entered the single room he heard Coyote mutter something about a bottle of Hostetter's Stomach Bitters.

'Feeling bilious, are you?' the druggist asked with professional interest as he reached up to a high shelf filled with bottles of just about every size and shape.

'Some,' Charlie Coyote agreed.

Sam took in the place at a glance. So far it was about the most permanent-looking business he'd seen in King Creek. Three of the four walls were covered in shelves, and the shelves were stocked with everything from Balm of Childhood and cathartic pills to Cuticura anti-pain plasters and vegetable worm-destroyer.

'Hurt your arm, I see,' said the druggist, ringing up one dollar on the till.

Coyote grunted a response and started to reach into his jacket pocket to pay for the tonic — which, like most such potions, was more alcohol than anything else. Sam drew his Remington and said, 'Don't move a muscle, Coyote. I got you covered.'

Charlie Coyote froze. Slowly his head came up and swiveled into profile. His dark, slightly glazed eyes shuttled around to fix on Sam's face.

'Wh . . . what is this — ?' asked the druggist in a reedy voice.

'I'm arrestin' you on suspicion of attempted murder, Charlie,' Sam snapped without preamble. 'Put your good hand up in the air an' don't go makin' this any trickier'n it has to be.'

'Now see here — ' said the druggist.

Sam ignored him. 'I'm waitin', Charlie.'

At last Charlie Coyote spoke. He said, 'Whatever it is you're gabbin' about, marshal, you're talkin' to the wrong feller about it here.'

'We can settle that once I got you

behind bars. Now get that arm up, away from yonder iron!'

To underline his words, he cocked the Remington. The sound was cold and loud.

Charlie Coyote thought about it some more as the druggist's saucer eyes travelled back and forth between them. At last the half-breed's shoulders dropped just a fraction and he said, 'All right, all right. Just don't get sudden with that cannon, marshal. I done told you I'm innocent.'

He started to raise his right hand, fingers splayed; and that's what he was doing when Tom MacLean, the one-armed, one-time blasting-engineer, stumbled through the doorway clutching what remained of the five dollars Randolph Stover's killer had given him the previous evening.

'B-b-bottle o' *Vin V-V-Vitae* when you're r-ready — '

It was about the only chance Coyote was going to get, and all he was likely to need. Even before MacLean had finished slurring his request, the half-breed's hand was streaking towards the Schofield riding his hip, and wheeling to confront the new marshal.

Sam, dropping to a crouch, yelled, '*Don't!*'

But Coyote ignored him. His first shot exploded bottles and tins from the shelves behind Sam. Fragments of glass flew through the air. The druggist disappeared behind his till and MacLean stood frozen in the doorway, watching events through bleary gray eyes, still too drunk to get out of the way.

Sam returned fire without having to think about it. Fragments of glass sparkled on his shoulders, and his buckskin jacket started to grow dark and patchy from the tonics splashed across it. His bullet missed its target but caused similar damage to the shelves behind Coyote, who started legging it over to the door.

The half-breed fired another shot. Sam went down flat as splinters burst from the edge of the counter. Coyote kept running. Sam came up and leveled the Remington on him.

'*Hold it!*'

But Coyote didn't hold it, and Sam knew that he couldn't risk another shot, because by then the half-breed and Tom MacLean were both wedged together in the doorway.

Sam straightened to his full height. He heard Coyote curse the one-armed man. Behind his till, the druggist was groaning over his ruined stock. Then Coyote pushed MacLean out of his way and the one-armed man blundered into Sam, bounced off and fell to his knees.

Quickly Sam hauled him back up. 'You all right?'

At first MacLean was addled. 'A-all right? Uh . . . s-s-sure . . . all r-r-right . . . '

That was all Sam wanted to hear. Leaving MacLean where he stood, he charged over to the door. Charlie Coyote was halfway across the street. He turned, leveled the Schofield and fired again. His bullet went wide. Sam's next shot kicked up dirt beside the half-breed's left boot.

Coyote spun away and began to pick up speed. An olive-green freight-wagon being hauled by four now-spooked team-horses came thundering towards him. The driver was fighting to engage the brake and bring the team under control, so far without success. Sam yelled for the half-breed to freeze, but he just kept going, too busy keeping Sam in his sights to see the oncoming danger.

At last the wagon-wheels began to lock, but the wall-eyed team kept straining at the leathers. Now the wagon-driver was yelling, too. Only when it seemed certain that the half-breed would vanish beneath the pounding hooves did Coyote think to pull his attention away from Sam.

He saw the freight-wagon bearing down on him and screamed. Up on the seat, the driver hauled mightily on the ribbons. Somehow the horses veered a couple of feet to the right, blurring past Coyote, who by now had frozen stiff in the middle of the street.

On the boardwalk, Sam heaved a sigh of relief. He guessed the sonofabitch must have a charmed life.

But then . . .

The wagon, being pulled off-course with its brakes still on, began to slur and skid. It started to swing around in an arc that would bring it parallel with the horses dragging it. A shudder went through its canvas cover. It started to tip onto its two left-side wheels —

There was a snapping sound as the wagon-tongue splintered. The horses, now free of the wagon's restraining weight, surged on down the street. With no other course of action left to him, the driver leapt from the seat and landed in a bruised heap.

The wagon itself smashed into Charlie Coyote and began to roll over with a series of weird, splintery shrieks. It bounced once, kept going, spilled its contents — an assortment of mining implements — and finally came to a halt thirty feet further along the street, wheels up and spinning.

Silence descended over the dusty scene, save for the distant thumping of the stamp-mills and the dull, buried thud of the underground blasters at work. Slowly the sidewalks began to fill with rubberneckers. Sam stepped down into the street, slipped his gun away and hustled over to the wagon-driver, who was sitting up and clutching one leg.

'Hold still there, friend,' Sam said, crouching beside him. 'You all right?'

The wagon-driver was a brawny man who now looked pale and trembly. 'Busted m'leg, feels like.'

Sam straightened up and stabbed a finger at the nearest watching towns-man. 'Go fetch a doctor, fast!'

The fellow took off at the double.

Sam picked his way through what remained of the wagon's scattered cargo at a more leisurely pace. Something told him there was no need to hurry. Finally he came to Charlie

Coyote. He didn't have to be a doctor to know that the half-breed was as dead as dogshit. The man looked broken in some places, flattened in others. Sam felt his gorge rise and turned away fast.

Up on the boardwalk someone said they just didn't know what things were coming to, what with the murder of Randolph Stover and all. Tom MacLean, standing beside the druggist in the apothecary store doorway, frowned.

'I-i-is that r-r-right? What th-they're sayin' 'bout R-R-Randolph Stover?' he asked.

The druggist looked decidedly ill. He didn't waste energy on words, just nodded.

MacLean's frown deepened. Something sluggish stirred in his memory . . . the previous night, a gunshot out near Stover's store . . . the dark alley in which he'd run into —

'Damn and blast it, MacLean! Will you just *look* at this mess!'

MacLean turned around. The druggist had gone back inside his store. The place smelled foul now, as one pungent chemical mixed with another. The druggist was shaking his head in despair, muttering something about people who just came in off the street and started shooting up a fellow's livelihood. At last he said, 'There's a bottle of tonic in it for you if you'll help me clean up.'

The offer made the one-armed man forget all about his hazy memories. He stepped into the apothecary store and nodded eagerly. 'S-s-sure . . . '

He gave no more thought to gunshots or murder — or the identity of Randolph Stover's killer.

6

'Well . . . ' Matt chewed doubtfully on his lower lip. 'I don't mind ridin' shotgun on Walt Sullivan's supply-wagons — so long as you figure you can handle things here.'

Sam regarded his son from behind the law office desk. It was late afternoon, about three hours since Charlie Coyote's death, and somehow Sam had straightened everything out. He'd had to deal with a deputation of the town council, of course, but he'd expected that. They were anxious. To them he was an unknown quantity. They wanted some reassurance that he didn't go shooting up every town he packed a badge in.

He'd told them straight; you didn't fry an egg without you cracked it open first. They couldn't expect him to lock horns with the Stovers or their hired guns and settle everything with a few quiet words. Like it or not, the situation would probably get worse before it got better.

To their credit, they'd accepted that.

Still, Charlie Coyote's death had left Sam sour in the guts. He'd been hoping to get a confession from the half-breed that would implicate the Stovers in his attempted murder of Jack Denton. Too bad that course of action was no longer a possibility.

There were, however, other matters to deal with, and high among them was the proposition Walt Sullivan had put to him earlier that day.

Matt seemed willing enough to troubleshoot for the young assayer's two supply-wagons, and Harrigan had agreed that it might be wisest for his health if he went along for the ride. The only question left to sort out was how they could cut the journey's risks to a minimum.

'From the sounds of it, too many people know about Sullivan's plans already,' Matt pointed out, flopping down onto the horsehair sofa. 'This feller Bryce Colbourne, who's puttin' up that block of stores, the men Sullivan's already asked to go to work for him . . . ' He shook his head, his long, youthful face troubled. 'I'd be mighty surprised if the Stovers didn't already know what he's figurin' to do.'

'I believe you're right,' Sam agreed. 'At first I reckoned this chore'd be straightforward, but the more I think on it, the more I'd say you can expect trouble *somewhere* along the line.'

'I'll be ready for it,' Matt replied confidently.

'*We'll* be ready for it,' said Harrigan, from behind the bars of the communal cell.

'Sure, sure.' Matt smiled, but it was obvious that his mind was elsewhere. After a moment he sighed. 'You know, I believe we could save considerable aggravation if we was to light out under cover of darkness, sometime soon.'

'How soon?'

Matt shrugged. 'Tonight? Say, around midnight?'

Sam sat up straight. 'That's not a bad idea. Not bad at *all*. It'd certainly box-up whatever plans the Stovers might've made.'

'That's what I thought.' He stood up and reached for his hat. 'Think I'll go put it to Sullivan. It's short notice, I know, but that's just the point.'

An hour later Matt was back. He closed the door behind him, took off his hat, went over to the coffee-pot and said, 'It's all fixed. Harrigan — we leave at midnight.'

★ ★ ★

Up in the family room of the fancy house on Crane Rock, Kate Stover stood with her head bowed in prayer. Before her, resting on two saw-horses, was a pine coffin with brass handles. The drapes had been drawn as a mark of respect for the deceased, and the family room was gray-blue and gloomy.

The mortician had only been able to do so much with Randolph's ruined face, so the coffin lid had already been screwed down. Now Kate's moist, chocolate-brown eyes strayed along its grainy length until they finally came to rest on a neat brass plaque.

RANDOLPH PHILLIP STOVER
1846–1881

Thirty-five years old, she thought. It was no age to die.

Her heart-shaped mouth tightened into a thin, angry line. She was not so much concerned with the *why* of her eldest son's death, only the identity of his killer. Randolph was in God's hands now, and beyond all further pain, but she . . . she ached inside, and craved revenge.

All the furniture had been shoved against the walls to make room for the coffin. Still more flowers had been placed on every available ledge. The air was stuffy, for the windows were closed, and powdery with the scents of the blooms. But Kate Stover seemed unaware of the close, cloying atmosphere. Her mind was elsewhere.

When the door behind her gave a small creak and swung open, she started, but regained her composure almost at once. She turned to face the newcomer, hands clasped in front of her flat stomach, the folds of her black dress rustling sharply.

Gene, her youngest son, stood in the doorway. He appeared in awe of his mother. Coming into the room, he closed the door softly behind him. His breathing was harsh and labored. The flowers were doing him no good at all. He coughed into the handkerchief clutched in his left hand.

'Well?' his mother asked quietly. 'What did you find out?'

Gene came over to the coffin. The mirror over the dead fireplace showed him his reflection; a skeletal-looking blond with a thin, pale face and sick brown eyes much older than his twenty-odd years.

'Whiteley did some checking,' Gene replied, keeping his voice low out of deference to his dead brother. 'It seems that this fellow Judge used to be quite a town-tamer. Even had dime novels written about him, too. Most recently he was the law in a little town called Austin Springs, Colorado. Now it seems he's a free agent.'

'He can't be bought,' Kate said as a statement.

'No, ma'am.'

'He's going to be a threat to us, then.'

Gene nodded. 'I should say so.'

'And that *other* matter?'

'Sullivan, you mean?'

His mother nodded.

'He definitely seems serious about this scheme to open a general store,' Gene reported, breaking off to cough some more into his handkerchief. 'I doubt he'll consider paying us our concession. He's got a stubborn streak, that man. He saw Judge earlier this afternoon, before all that to-do with

Charlie Coyote, and not so long ago Judge's deputy also paid him a visit. I should say they've been discussing Sullivan's plan at some length, and intend to do something about it — soon.'

He coughed into his handkerchief again.

Kate nodded. 'He'll need supplies before he can open a store,' she mused softly. For a moment she was silent, her head bowed in thought. Then she fixed Gene with her firm, direct gaze. 'Fetch Dale,' she said.

Gene stayed where he was. 'I'll handle it, Mother. No need to trouble Dale. Just tell me what you want done.'

His mother's voice was flat. 'Fetch Dale,' she repeated.

Anger flared in his tired brown eyes for a moment, but he knew better than to argue the point. Even though Randolph had been taken from them, he was still being regarded as the kid of the family; worse, as the *sick* kid. He wanted to tell his mother that he was a man now, that she should entrust to him a man's duties. But all he did was nod slowly, say, 'Yes, Mother,' and leave the room.

★　★　★

Later that evening, Matt and Harrigan bedded down in the large cell and caught up on their sleep. For them it was going to be a long night, and they would need all their wits about them.

Sam stood out on the office porch, enjoying the cool night air. It was sometime around eight o'clock, and the sky was just turning from purple to starry black. There was nothing particularly comforting about the peace which had settled across the town, though. If anything, it was ominous; the calm before the storm.

But it figured. This was a Stover town, so the town had to show a little respect for the Stover who'd passed on. Dale's *Pot of Gold* was closed for the night, and whether they liked it or not, so was every other saloon and fun-house in King Creek. Only the pounding stamp-mills broke the eerie silence, and even they would be shutting down for the night soon.

Sam took out a cigar and lit up. His fat Abyssinian cat, Mitzi, circled his legs, seeking attention. The cat had been missing all day, no doubt familiarizing herself with her new environs. Now she had come home, hungry, thirsty and craving affection.

Sam bent down and scooped the animal up. Idly he scratched her head and ears. She squeezed her sea-green eyes shut in ecstasy. For so long, back in Austin Springs, it had been just Mitzi and him. Then his son had come along, and together they'd shaken the dust of Colorado from their heels.

Not that Sam regretted the leaving. It was just that he'd been alone for so long, he just wasn't used to worrying over kin.

And the more he thought about the trip to Dalhart and back, the more he felt that Matt would run into trouble. Part of him regretted involving the boy in Sullivan's scheme; another part told him he couldn't wrap Matt in cotton-wool — and that he shouldn't even try.

He turned and walked back into the office, closing the door on the silence outside. Putting the tan-and-white cat down, he rummaged around for a saucer, into which he poured some water. 'You'll eat when we get back to Pearl's,' he promised softly. The cat lapped at the water.

Anyway, Sam reasoned, if what Sullivan said was true, Matt would be in good company. The men he'd hired to drive his wagons were trail-wise and honest, by all accounts. They'd seen action during the war, too, so at least they knew one end of a gun from the other. He also felt that Harrigan could be relied upon.

He still couldn't help worrying, though.

At eleven o'clock he roused the sleeping men and brewed some fresh coffee while they saw to their ablutions out in the moon-washed backyard. Half an hour later they were ready to say their farewells. Sam watched them mount up at the hitch-rack, Matt aboard his wiry little cow-pony, Harrigan astride a rented *grulla*.

There was a round of handshakes, and an exchange of heartfelt good-lucks. Then Matt and Harrigan rode off down Main in the direction of Sullivan's tent, where the assayer, his wagons and their drivers would be waiting.

Sam felt hollow and weary. It had, after all, been a long day. He took one last look around the office, then blew out the lamps. Outside, he locked up the jail, slipped the cat into one of his saddlebags, climbed aboard his roan and set off in the opposite direction.

The trip out to Pearl's place was quiet and uneventful. A homely yellow glow showed at one of the windows, where the drapes hadn't quite been drawn shut. Sam dismounted, led his horse out back, off-saddled and saw to its comfort. By the time he carried Mitzi back around front, he found Pearl waiting for him in the doorway.

'Thought I heard you ride up,' she said. As he followed her inside and closed the door behind him, she threw a glance over her shoulder. 'Hungry, Sam? I got some stew and dumplings left over that won't take but a minute to hot up.'

He set the cat down and nodded. 'Thanks.'

While she busied herself at the range, he took a seat at the table. The single room was lit by two guttering oil-lamps, and every corner held a dancing shadow. 'Where's Jack?' he asked.

'Where else?' she replied with an edge to her voice. 'Sleepin'.'

Sam grunted, sensing her disquiet, but refrained from further comment.

'Talkin' of wheres,' the fat woman asked as she stirred the contents of a big, fire-blackened pot, 'where's Matt?'

With a heavy sigh he told her.

At once she forgot all about her own problems and came over to study him with concern on her heavily-painted face. 'You're worried about him,' she said.

'Some.'

'Do you think you've got good reason?'

He shrugged. 'I'd say there's a pretty fair chance he'll run into trouble, yeah.'

'How long do you figure he'll be gone?'

He ran long fingers over his stubbly chin. 'Dalhart's a hundred an' sixty mile round trip. With heavy-loaded wagons, maybe a fortnight.'

She nodded, turned and heaved herself back over to the range. 'I wouldn't worry overmuch if I was you,' she said to encourage him. 'I know I've only just met him, but Matt strikes me as the type who can take care of himself.' She gave the pot one more stir, then turned and looked straight into Sam's face. 'In fact, he kind of reminds me of you,' she added meaningfully.

Sam kept a poker face. 'That's another thing,' he said to change the subject. 'I'm no nearer to collaring this here killer we've got runnin' around town.'

She ladled stew into a bowl and brought it over. Steam rose off it invitingly. Sam took the spoon she proffered and set to, keeping his eyes on the meal, not on her.

'Sam,' she began cautiously, sitting opposite him. 'About Matt . . . '

'Yeah?'

'You must be awful proud of him.'

He nodded. 'He's a good feller to ride the river with.'

'That's not what I mean,' she said.

He met her gaze and said, 'I know.'

She threw a dispirited look around the room. 'Never did have any kids of my own.'

'That's too bad.'

'It is. But then again, maybe it's a blessin'. To be spared all the worry of 'em, I mean.'

He chewed on a dumpling, feeling

awkward in front of this woman who'd damn'-near broke his heart all those years before.

'I guess I'm gonna go and make a fool of myself now,' she said with a little self-conscious laugh. 'But what the hell. It's just that seein' you again's made me think of all those high times we knew back in 'Frisco.'

She reached across the table and closed her right hand over his left. He looked up and saw tears moving around in her piggy green eyes.

'Don't get me wrong now,' she said in a soft but urgent voice. 'I wouldn't do a thing to hurt Jack but . . . ah, hell . . . I'm still a *woman*, Sam . . . and you and me, there always *was* somethin' special between us . . . '

He dropped his spoon into the bowl with a rattle that shattered the moment. 'That's right,' he said, speaking before he gave thought to what he was saying. 'There was. But as I recall, there was somethin' a damn' sight more special between you an' that feller I used to call a partner.'

She stared at him with her mouth open in surprise. A tear slid down one rouged cheek in a series of stops and starts. She took her hand away from his and nodded. 'Yeah,' she said quietly. 'I guess there was.'

Angry with himself, he pushed his chair back and stood up. 'Hell, I'm sorry, Pearl. I didn't mean — '

'It's all right.'

'No it's not, dammit! But it's been a long day, an' I've been set upon, shot at, an' watched a feller get squashed by a two-ton freight-wagon. I'm tired as hell, Pearl, an' frettin' like a mother hen about Matt.'

'I know.'

He came around the table and reached down to cup her double chin. At first she refused to take her eyes away from her lap. Then she looked up at him.

'But apart from all that,' he said, calming down, 'memories of 'Frisco are all you 'n' me've got left. Times change, girl. *People* change. An' like it or not, you can't go back.' He knelt beside her. 'You're a swell lady, Pearl, an' don't ever think otherwise. But you're a married woman, an' you've got a sick husband who needs all the love you can give him,' he said gently. 'Happen we did anythin' rash tonight, we'd wake up hatin' ourselves for it in the mornin'. You *know* we would.'

She nodded. 'Happen you're right,' she said softly. 'I . . . y-yeah . . . Happen you're right.'

But she didn't sound thoroughly convinced.

And for that matter, neither did Sam.

★　★　★

Mid-morning of the next day, Matt called a halt up on some high ground littered with ocotillo and barrel cactus typical of that south-eastern quarter of Nevada. The drivers of the two supply-wagons, Bates and Seagrave, hauled back on their reins and kicked down on their brakes. The four-horse teams came to a halt and the Conestogas stalled there amid the cholla, saguaro and wind-eroded rocks.

'Thirty-minute break,' Matt announced, hipping around in his saddle.

'About time,' Bates grumbled. 'I bin sweatin' like a pig up here.'

'Sure is hot,' Seagrave remarked, unstoppering a canteen and tilting his head back to drink.

It was. Riding drag, Harrigan's thin, ruddy face was glistening with sweat, and his blue eyes were narrowed against the harsh sun-glare bouncing up off the dusty, arid terrain surrounding them. He estimated it to be maybe ninety-five in the shade, though it would grow cooler once they entered the hills running north to south directly ahead. The horses were dusted with salt, and the men weren't much better. They'd made good time since their midnight departure from King Creek, but now they all needed a rest.

Bates and Seagrave hopped down

from their wagon-seats. Both men were big-bellied and bearded, with sun-reddened faces half-hidden by the broad brims of their black felt hats. Bates was maybe forty, Seagrave a decade older. Both men were thick-armed and tall. They moved the way muscular men always moved, like hulking brutes, but there was nothing brutal about their personalities. Both Matt and Harrigan had found them to be amiable and willing, albeit a little edgy about the job at hand.

Matt dismounted and tied his pony's reins to a nearby growth of brittlebrush. He'd been riding out ahead of the wagons with his Winchester across his pommel while Harrigan rode drag. Even now he carried the long-gun, and kept his eyes busy on their apparently peaceful surroundings.

'Here,' said Seagrave, tossing him a small sack of jerky. 'He'p y'self.'

'Thanks.' Matt delved into the sack, pulled out a twisted stick of dried beef and passed it back to the wagon-driver.

A faint, welcome breeze blew up as he took off his hat and ran a shirtsleeve across his forehead. He noticed that Harrigan was still sitting astride his *grulla* in the ruts left by the two wagons, his attention focused on their back-trail.

'We got time to coffee 'n' cake ourselves, Matt?' Bates asked, stretching. 'Properly, I mean.'

Matt began to loosen his horse's cinch-strap. 'Sure, why not?'

'I'll see to it,' said Seagrave. 'I've got a skillet an' some bacon in my possibles.'

By the time Harrigan joined Matt over by the shade cast by the rocks, the younger man was stretched out on the ground with his hat tilted over his eyes.

Harrigan, watching him, gave a small, incredulous laugh. 'Sure, an' I thought you'd take your shotgun-ridin' duties a little more seriously than this!' he said.

Matt pushed his hat back and squinted up at him. 'I am, believe me. But if there's one thing I've learned since I've been ridin' with Sam, it's how to think like the *other* sonofabitch.'

Harrigan joined him on the ground. 'Oh? An' how do you suppose the other sonofabitch is thinkin' right now?' he asked.

Matt sniffed. 'Well, if there *are* any Stover men out there — and we're not even sure that there *are* — I'd say they're bidin' their time.'

Harrigan frowned. 'Waitin' to find the best place to ambush us, is that what you mean?'

'Waitin' for the right *moment*,' Matt corrected.

'Which is . . . ?'

'Lessen I miss my guess, once we've collected all of Sullivan's supplies an're well on our way back to King Creek.'

Harrigan digested that, then saw the logic of it. 'By cracky, Matt, I'd say you're right! The crafty bastards! If they could only pull it off, they'd box-up Sullivan's plans to open a store, *and* get 'emselves two wagonloads of supplies free into the bargain!'

'Well, that's how *I* figure it. But I don't intend to take anythin' for granted. 'Far as I can see, there's nobody doggin' us — but that don't mean a thing.'

'Sure, sure. But it wouldn't surprise me one bit if you haven't called it right, me boy. Stover's bullies'll wait until we're loaded down with supplies,' Harrigan said, nodding, '*then* they'll hit us, nothin' surer.'

★   ★   ★

For the next couple of days, nothing of much consequence happened in King Creek. Randolph Stover's general store opened up with Dick Whiteley in residence. Randolph himself was planted not far from the house on Crane Rock just as soon as the circuit preacher came through town and performed the service. The stamp-mills kept on pounding, the blasters kept on blasting and the miners kept on mining.

But Sam found it difficult to settle

into a routine. For one thing, he still had himself a killer to find, and he was making precious little progress in that direction. For another, he was beginning to have Pearl's unsavory stories about Dale's saloon, the *Pot of Gold*, verified by disgruntled miners.

Thus it was that he stopped off at the Stover watering-hole sometime around eight o'clock one cloudy Wednesday evening, just to see for himself if what they said about moonshine whiskey and rigged games of chance was true.

The saloon was doing hellish good business as he stepped through the batwings, but that came as no surprise. The Stovers had limited their competition strictly, making sure that there were only so many places a body could go to find some cheer. More than a hundred miner-types were jammed up along the thirty-foot mahogany bar, and perhaps a hundred more were sitting at the tables lining each wall, or crowding around the two roulette wheels.

The air was smoky and stale. The

saloon stank of kerosene and booze. A Pianola tinkled out one melody after another. Behind the counter, three bartenders in shirtsleeves and bow ties worked flat-out dispensing drinks, and just right of the bar a staircase swept up to a grand-looking gallery where percentage girls called down lewd invitations to the potential marks below.

Sam let the batwings swing shut behind him and shouldered through the throng. The walls held all manner of paintings and mirrors, which gave the saloon a look of elegance. The sounds of chatter, laughter and clinking glass cheapened the place, however, and when he finally found a space at the bar he had to shout to make himself heard.

'Whiskey!'

The nearest bartender followed his initial glance at Sam with a double-take. But the man's vaguely bloodshot eyes didn't linger so much on his face as his shield.

Within a moment he recovered

himself. 'Uh . . . sure, marshal. Comin' up!'

He reached beneath the counter, then froze when Sam leaned forward and clamped a hand around his wrist. 'Not the good stuff,' he said. 'The panther-piss you serve to all these *other* fellers.'

The bartender was youngish, maybe late twenties, with a florid face and a waxed moustache. He looked Sam straight in the face, indecision plain in his sore-looking eyes. Eventually he pulled an unmarked bottle off the back shelf and spilled amber liquid into a smeared shot glass. 'H-here,' he said. 'On the house.'

'I'll pay for it,' Sam said in a flat tone.

The bartender nodded. 'As you will,' he replied in a sullen tone. 'That'll be fifty cents.'

A man next to Sam, who'd been listening to the exchange, snorted indignantly. 'Well, that's rich! You buy a whiskey an' Corbett here charges you fifty cents. I buy the self-same drink an' pay the full dollar!'

Sam threw him a glance. He saw a tall, clean-shaven man with a wall eye, maybe Sam's own age. 'I'd say that's one good reason to go drink someplace else,' he said. Raising his glass, he sniffed at the contents. He took a cautious sip, then spat it out. He'd tasted potato peelings, hair-oil, caramel for coloring and other things he couldn't put a name to, but nothing of real whiskey at all, just pure bust-head — sometimes lethal moonshine.

Suddenly he grew aware of electricity filling the air, and knew that trouble was coming.

'Give me that bottle,' he told the bartender, Corbett.

'Huh . . . what — '

'Give me the bottle!' Sam barked.

Corbett hopped to it, his florid face coloring even more now that the new marshal's shenanigans were beginning to draw the attention of the other patrons lining the bar.

He grabbed the bottle, turned back

to Sam and thrust it forward. Sam took it by the neck and said thanks, then turned around just as a giant in a brown tweed suit lumbered up with 'bouncer' written all over him.

'You got a problem here, marshal?' the bouncer asked in a voice like shifting gravel.

Sam shook his head. 'Not anymore.'

He brought the bottle up and smashed it alongside the bouncer's head, not so much to incapacitate the fellow as to get the attention of the other drinkers. Glass shattered and the pungent moonshine splashed across the bouncer's lumpy face. The man went down in a heap and stayed there.

Virtually all eyes had now been drawn to the trouble occurring up at the bar. Even the percentage girls had focused their attention on the grizzled lawman.

'Someone turn off that piano!' Sam bellowed, tossing the neck of the bottle away.

Someone did.

'That's better,' Sam said into the silence.

He heard footsteps coming from upstairs and craned his neck just as Dale Stover pushed through the knot of sporting girls clustered along the gallery. The dandy of the family wore a look of irritation on his long, tanned face. He was dressed much as he had been the first time Sam had seen him, in a black Prince Albert and tight gray pants, but now his shirt was open at the collar and his macassared brown hair was mussed. Sam had the feeling that he'd interrupted Dale from something more physical than office work, and smiled.

'What — ' Dale's brown eyes grew sharp as they focused on Sam. He pushed away from the gallery rail and came halfway down the stairs, anger tightening his high, prominent cheekbones and pinching at his straight nose and narrow, lemony lips. 'Just what is it you think you're playing at, Judge?' he demanded.

'It's called my duty,' Sam replied easily. 'You've reigned for long enough, Stover. It's about time someone spoke up for these poor dumb miners you keep fleecin'.'

Dale treated him to a blunt and unflattering evaluation. At length he smiled. 'And you're it, are you?'

Sam nodded. 'I'm it,' he replied. 'An' I'm closin' you down, as of right now.'

'*What?*'

'Might've escaped your notice,' Sam said into the sudden babble of excited conversation, 'but they got ordinances here that folks're expected to abide by. You're breakin' Lord alone knows how many.'

'Ah, don't hand me that — '

'You're sellin' bust-head whiskey that's strong enough to blind or kill,' Sam cut in relentlessly. 'You're chargin' well over the odds for it, too. An' as for your games of chance . . . '

He pushed through the rest of the patrons until he came to one of the roulette wheels. Before anyone could stop him, he grabbed the edge of the baize-topped table and lifted. The table went over with a crash. Paper money and colored chips scattered across the floor. Again a buzz of surprise went through the crowd. Then Sam grabbed one edge of the canvas sheet tacked across the underside of the table and ripped it back to expose the workings of the wheel — the wheel and the thin wires and pulleys attached to it that, when operated correctly, guaranteed better than fair odds in favor of the house.

Silence fell over the big, bright room.

Sam turned to slant a withering stare up into Dale's furious face. 'If you like, I'll quote you chapter an' verse,' he said.

Dale's response was a sneer. 'I don't think that'll be necessary.'

'I didn't think it would, somehow. Now move along, folks. This place is closin' down until such time as I've figured out all the fines that need payin'. In any case, I'd say there's better saloons to waste your money in than this'un.'

There were one or two small sounds of protest from the back of the room, but for the most part the now-subdued patrons began to shuffle toward the door, some of the bolder ones stooping to help themselves to the scattered cash and chips.

'Judge.'

Sam glanced up at Dale.

'You'll be sorry for this,' Dale Stover said gravely. 'I promise you.'

'You try mixin' it with me,' Sam replied, 'an' you'll be runnin' this place through bandages.'

As he saw the last of the patrons out, he was smiling.

7

Ten o'clock next morning there was a sharp, business-like rap at the law office door, and Sam, who'd been sweeping the floor, looked up just as Kate Stover came into the large room and closed the portal behind her.

Outside the sky was gray and overcast, and the air had a clammy feel of humidity about it. A storm was coming, nothing surer; and from the look on Kate Stover's face, there was going to be another kind of storm preceding it.

Sam nodded a greeting. He'd half-expected a visit like this; after all, he'd closed down the *Pot of Gold* specifically to force the Stovers into some form of retaliation. Now he set the broom aside and came around his desk.

'Mornin', ma'am.'

'Marshal,' she replied with a stiff nod

that sent a shiver through her ash-blonde curls.

'This *is* a surprise,' he lied. 'May I ask to what do I owe the honor?'

A faint, mocking smile touched her heart-shaped lips and lit a small fire in her bright, direct brown eyes. 'Your performance last night,' she replied bluntly. 'As if you didn't know.'

Sam feigned puzzlement. 'Performance?' he echoed. 'I disremember any kind of performance. What'd I do? Sing? Dance? Tell witticisms?'

'Let's not play games,' she snapped. 'I'll be frank with you, marshal. Dale was all for having that smile slapped right off your face. I, on the other hand, hope to be a little more reasonable.' She held up a tiny purse of the same crushed blue velvet as the two-piece jacket and skirt she was wearing over her crisp white blouse. 'In short, I'm here to settle whatever fines you've decided to impose.'

Sam rubbed his chin. 'Fair enough. Have a seat while I figure it all out.'

'No thank you.'

He shrugged. 'Coffee, then?'

'This isn't a social call,' she reminded him.

Her eyes strayed to the empty cell at the rear of the office and something unpleasant came into her face. 'Where is my son's killer?' she asked.

Sam gave another shrug. 'I wish I knew. But believe me, I'm workin' on it, ma'am, an' as soon as I find the miscreant responsible — '

'I'm referring to Harrigan,' she said through gritted teeth. 'The man you were *supposed* to be holding in custody.'

Sam threw a glance over his shoulder. 'Oh, him. Well, he's still in custody, ma'am, you can be sure of that.'

'*Whose* custody?'

'My deputy's.'

'And where is your deputy?'

'Out of town at present.'

'On business?'

'Uh-huh.'

'This business,' she said. 'Where does

Harrigan fit into it?'

'He doesn't. But judging by the behavior of your two lapdogs Coltrain and Baker, I'd say he's a sight safer where he is right now than he would be locked up in here. He's only a *suspect*, after all, ma'am. We don't know for sure that he's the feller we want.'

She sneered at him. 'Wouldn't you say you're exceeding your authority just a little?' she asked. 'Allowing the man to go free?'

He smiled sweetly. 'If you're not happy about it,' he replied, 'you can always call in a U.S. Marshal.'

She made no response, so he went back around the desk. Mitzi was curled up asleep in his Douglas chair. He lifted her up and set her down on the floor. She yawned, slunk over to the horsehair sofa, leapt up onto it and settled down to continue her shut-eye.

As Sam picked up a stub of pencil and started to make a column of figures, he heard Kate Stover make a few small sounds of impatience. Good.

He'd wanted to irritate her, because it seemed there were so few who'd ever dare.

At last he said, 'Hmm. Let's say an even hundred bucks, shall we? For the fine?'

Her face betrayed nothing. 'Very well.' She opened the purse and delved inside. With great deliberation she counted five-dollar bills out in front of him. Her eyes never left his face, but if she was hoping for some kind of reaction, she was disappointed. He'd never been a particularly avaricious man.

'Just hold on a minute an' I'll give you a receipt,' he said when she'd finished.

She closed the purse. 'You know, the money you see there is *nothing*, Marshal Judge, *nothing*, compared to what you *could* earn as a member of my staff.'

His mild gray eyes glittered with amusement as he signed the scribbled receipt with a flourish. 'I don't suppose it is,' he agreed, getting up and coming back around the desk to hand her the counterfoil. 'But I believe I've already told you once that I can't be bought off.'

'Pride is one thing,' she said. 'Downright stupidity is something else.' She looked up into his face and he smelled the faint, womanly perfume of her. 'We're here to stay, marshal, what remains of my family and I,' she said in a low voice. 'We won't be driven out by *anyone*. The fools who attempt to defy us are either *bought* off, or *killed* off. Do I make myself clear?'

'Yes'm. But now let me make myself clear. Toe the line an' you'll find me an easy enough feller to get along with. Keep tryin' to rule the good folks of this town with your bully-boy tactics an' I'll crush you all. You, Dale an' Gene.'

She glared up into his face, then moved, suddenly, her right hand blurring up to slap him across the cheek.

He caught her by the wrist and

tightened his fingers around her soft, pale skin. 'I wouldn't advise assaultin' a duly-deputized officer of the law, ma'am,' he said, deadpan. 'I'd have to put you behind bars pendin' trial, an' while it might be true that you sure look good in blue, I doubt you'd look half so fetchin' in prison-gray.'

Again he caught a faint waft of her perfume. It surprised him that he should find the nearness of her exciting, and the fire in her eyes so attractive. But what surprised him even more was the revelation that the feeling was evidently mutual.

With an effort Kate Stover moved back a step, and he released his grip on her wrist. She put the receipt in her purse, snapped it shut and took another pace away from him. She was flustered, obviously not used to losing control of either situations or emotions.

'I don't relish the prospect of locking horns with you,' she said at the door. 'But neither will I shy away when the time finally comes for our showdown.'

Then she was gone, slamming the door behind her.

* * *

'Well?' asked Matt. 'All done?'

Seagrave dipped his shaggy head twice. His smile was wide enough to cut his bushy beard in two. 'Yep. Got just about ever'thin' on Sullivan's list from cut plug to Heinz preserves, in the right quantities an' at the right prices.' The big wagon-driver hooked a thumb over his shoulder at the large, brick-built store rising behind him. 'Bates is just takin' the wagons around back now. I'd say they'll be loaded an' ready to go by three o'clock.'

'Good work.'

Around them, the town of Dalhart fairly buzzed with commerce. Matt and the others had arrived late the previous evening, and set up a temporary camp on some disused parkland on the north-east fringes of town. While Bates stayed behind to keep watch with a

Henry repeater in his gnarled fists, the others had taken a turn around town, searching for the supplier to whom Walt Sullivan had addressed his order.

That Dalhart was a prosperous community soon became obvious. There was nothing of mud-splattered canvas here; the buildings were all log- or brick-built, and the stores, of which there seemed an endless variety, appeared grand with their false fronts and bright window displays. The citizens, too, lacked that rough-and-ready appearance so common in King Creek. These were folks who'd put down roots; not drifters forever in search of a bonanza.

After locating the store they were after, Matt, Harrigan and Seagrave had eaten a late supper at a steam-filled chow-house on Front Street, then returned to the wagons. The night had passed uneventfully, as indeed had the entire eighty-mile trip, and first thing this morning, Bates and Seagrave had set about acquiring the supplies Sullivan had listed.

For a moment, just looking up and down Front Street, Matt felt that perhaps everything would turn out all right. He'd maintained a close watch on their back-trail and seen no-one and nothing save the seemingly endless wastes. Still, he knew better than to grow complacent. It was from this moment on that a possible attack by Stover men would be most likely.

'Right,' he said, snapping out of his reverie. 'Happen you've got things under control here, I think I'll go get my hair c — what's wrong?'

A change had come over Seagrave's face, and his deep, dark eyes, now focused on something beyond Matt's left shoulder, had narrowed to slits. 'Well I'll be damned . . . ' he muttered.

Matt stiffened. 'What — '

'No, don't turn 'round! Let's not tip our hand.'

Matt nodded, fighting his natural impulse to follow Seagrave's gaze. 'What is it, then?' he asked in a low, tense voice.

'You know Johnny Baker?'

'We've met. He's a Stover man.'

'He's up on yonder boardwalk, watchin' us.'

'You're sure?'

'Pretty certain. Wait a second . . . he's turnin' away now . . . yeah . . . most likely reportin' back to whoever he's brought along with him.'

Matt said, 'Damn. He still in sight?'

Seagrave shook his head. 'Not any more. Just went into yonder beer-house.'

At last Matt turned around and aimed his gray gaze at a saloon halfway along the opposite boardwalk that called itself Bodeen's.

For an instant he considered going over there himself and bracing the Stover hard case. Then he hesitated. That he and the others would have trouble somewhere along the trail back to King Creek now seemed almost certain. But if Matt could only work it so that the trouble occurred at the time and place of *his* choosing . . .

He turned back to Seagrave, an idea already taking form in his mind. 'All right . . . Tell 'em to take their time loadin' the wagons. We won't be movin' out 'till after dark.'

'Huh — ?'

'Trust me.' Now Matt's mind was racing on ahead. 'An' keep your long-gun handy while I go find Harrigan an' tell him what I plan to do . . . '

* * *

Harrigan didn't like it. He didn't like it at all. 'Saints alive, Matt, I might be many things, but a killer's not one of 'em.'

Matt eyed him steadily. 'Not even to save your own skin?'

Harrigan glanced away. 'Well . . . '

'Anyway, it might not come to killin', though I'd say it probably will. Baker an' whoever he's got with him'll see to that.'

The ruddy-faced miner chewed worriedly at his lower lip. Matt had caught up with him out at the clearing where they'd made camp.

Harrigan had been seeing to the care of his horse when Matt rode up, dismounted and quickly filled him in on what had happened.

Now he watched the Irishman's thin, weathered face closely, his worried blue eyes too, and knew without any shadow of a doubt that never in a thousand years could he have murdered Randolph Stover.

'Well?' he prompted quietly.

Harrigan met his eyes and gave a fatalistic shrug. 'You an' Marshal Judge've treated me pretty decently,' he said, cracking a sour, apprehensive smile. 'I reckon it's about time I did somethin' to repay that.'

Matt released his pent-up breath. If necessary, he'd have gone ahead with his plan alone, as difficult as that might've worked out. At least with Harrigan along, the odds didn't look so bad. 'All right. Here's how we're gonna do it . . . '

* * *

When darkness spread across the land Matt told the others to get ready to move out. Bates and Seagrave, both veterans of the War Between the States but basically men of peace, climbed aboard their Conestogas with a heavy sense of foreboding in their chests. Harrigan, riding point, swung into his saddle and urged his *grulla* to a walk. In the deep shadows out back of the now-closed supply-store it was difficult to tell for sure, but Matt, who'd elected to ride drag, was almost certain he'd seen the Irishman's thin lips moving in silent prayer.

Harrigan led them along the moon-washed alley between the store and the building next to it, then swung his horse left, out onto Front Street. Behind him the wagons emerged one at a time from the shadows, rattling and creaking, their canvas covers shivering and shifting to the motion of the slowly-turning wheels.

Matt was the last one out of the alley.

Front Street was much quieter now than it had been that morning. Most of the stores were either closed for the night or just in the process of closing. Matt saw a few townsfolk hurrying back and forth along the boardwalk, but none of them paid much attention to his slow-moving column.

Dalhart had three saloons. On their way out of town, the wagons trundled past all of them. Light spilled yellow and inviting from the windows and from above and beneath the batwing doors, falling in puddles on the weathered boardwalks and silver-filled horse-troughs.

They rode on out of town, into the darkness.

The road was wide and uneven. It curved this way and that through land stubbled with spindly ocotillo and drab, olive-green tufts of grass. The trail was rutted from the passage of much traffic. Moonlight splashed off the seamed rocks that began rising up on either side of them. Out ahead, maybe four or six miles away, lay the foothills out of which they'd come barely twenty-four hours earlier. And beyond the foothills rose the cool brown mountains, black now, and ragged against the starry purple sky.

A tarantula scuttled across the trail up ahead. Matt spotted it easily in the pale moon-glow. It disappeared beneath the wagon in front of him, then came out on the other side, moving faster and with purpose.

They rode on.

Matt checked the darkness behind them. He felt sure that Baker and whoever else the Stovers had sent after them were out there somewhere. They *must* be, for they would almost certainly have set someone to keep an eye on them. But they wouldn't make a move yet; they were still too close to town, and gunfire might bring unwelcome attention. Give it another few miles, say just as they started up into the foothills, and then . . .

Half an hour later Matt spotted the stand of juniper, spiky sotol plants and low rocks he'd chosen for their rearguard action. If Harrigan was awake and following orders, he should have turned off at this point, tied his *grulla* someplace out of sight and picked himself a good spot from which to make a fight of it.

The wagons rattled on with nary a pause. Bates and Seagrave both had their orders; to keep going no matter what. Matt reined in, hipped around, strained his eyes to find any sign that might confirm whether or not the men who meant them harm were out there.

He saw nothing.

Hauling his Winchester from its sheath, he sent the cow-pony on up the trail, then off to the right and in among the rocks and foliage. Shadows clung to the spot. He dismounted, listening to the wagons moving away into the star-picked gloom.

'Harrigan?'

It was a sibilant whisper.

'Here.'

Matt followed the voice over to a jumble of low rocks twelve feet away. He noted at once that the spot afforded the Irishman a good view of the trail they'd just travelled. Harrigan was sprawled behind the rocks with the Winchester he'd taken from the gun-rack back at the King Creek law office in his hands.

Matt glanced around. Harrigan had tied his *grulla* to a juniper tree well back from his position. Quickly Matt led his own horse to the same spot, tethered it and came back.

Hunkering down beside his companion, he said, 'I hope you're a patient man. We could be here for quite a while.'

Harrigan muttered something under his breath.

'What was that?'

The Irishman looked over at him. 'I just said you're takin' an awful lot for granted. About Baker, I mean. What's to say he hasn't already quit town, an' found a place somewhere up *ahead* to set his trap?'

Matt shook his head, trying to dispel his own last-minute doubts. 'Just a hunch. I doubt the sonofabitch would want to let us out of his sight for *too* long.'

'Even so — '

'*Shhh!*'

'Eh?'

'Listen!'

They both heard it then; the sound of hoof beats, muffled by distance — but coming steadily closer along their shadowy back-trail.

★   ★   ★

Sam was about halfway through his last patrol of the evening when the heavens opened up. Within moments King Creek was caught beneath a veritable deluge. Rain slanted down across the mismatched tents and wood-built stores. It rattled on porch overhangs, drummed against canvas, turned the narrow streets to mud and needled each fast-filling puddle with a thousand liquid darts. Overhead the sky lit up. A moment later thunder bellowed its accompanying roar.

Sam went from a slow walk to a fast run, stopping only when he found shelter in a half-built store midway along Main. Even though he'd only been out in it for maybe thirty seconds, he was already drenched. Leaning up against a wall, he shook his arms, flicking beads of water off his fingertips, then fished around in his jacket pocket for a damp cigar.

Lighting up, he surveyed the street through a haze of smoke. Although it was nearly midnight, life in the saloons and bawdy-houses was still getting along at a fair clip. For the most part, however, the streets were empty — as indeed had been Dale Stover's *Pot of Gold*.

A faint smile touched his lips as he remembered stopping by the newly-reopened drinking-parlor just fifteen minutes earlier. The two-hundred-strong crowd of the previous night now numbered no more than fifty. The three bartenders looked dispirited. The roulette wheels were shunned. If trade grew much worse, Sam reflected with grim satisfaction, the percentage girls would soon outnumber the customers.

Again lightning flickered across the sky. Maybe this storm would clear the air at last. Sam puffed more smoke into the moist night air as his thoughts turned to Matt.

He wondered how his boy was doing, way out there to the south and east. He realized how much he missed Matt's company, and it surprised him, for he'd always been something of a lone wolf before. *Must be gettin' old*, he thought. *Old an' foolish*.

The half-built frame around him trembled to the next clap of thunder, but at least the rain was starting to ease up. The next rumble of thunder came from somewhere off to the north, and the flashes of lightning began to grow increasingly intermittent. The cloud-burst was passing over.

When the rain had died down to a steady drizzle, Sam tossed the cigar away and continued on his way. He'd finish his patrol, then go to bed down back at the office.

He was just crossing a shadowy alley-mouth when he heard something that made him turn and peer into the darkness. Sounded like someone in pain.

With the short hairs at the base of his neck stirring faintly, he let his right hand brush the grips of his holstered Remington. 'Anyone there?' he asked into the darkness.

He heard the soft groaning sound again.

His eyes narrowed. 'Who is it?'

There was no reply, but now that the hiss of the rain was dying away, he could hear other sounds; harsh breathing, the small noises someone in there was making trying to get up.

He took a pace into the alley-mouth,

his eyes slowly adjusting to the gloom. A watery moon was reflected in the puddles scattered along the narrow thoroughfare. Scudding clouds kept affecting the level of light. Then Sam discerned a figure no more than a dozen feet away, curled up against the left-side wall. He hustled over and knelt beside it.

'It's all right, feller . . . '

'Uh . . . '

Sam reached down, intending to turn the figure over. The hunched shape was shivering and his clothes were sodden. Sam closed his fingers around the man's shoulders, then recoiled, more in surprise than revulsion, as he realized that the fellow was missing his right arm.

At last he turned the man onto his back. The night's silence was filled with heavy breathing and the steady drip-drip of water falling off porch overhangs and slanted roofs. He looked into the shivering man's face and saw glassy gray eyes, a lumpy, drinker's nose, a slack, open mouth and a round, stubbly chin.

The fellow seemed familiar. Then he had it. It was the one-armed man he'd collided with down at the apothecary store during his brief to-do with Charlie Coyote.

He smelled strong tonic on the man's breath, but guessed by the intensity of his tremors that something else was ailing him. 'You got a name, friend?'

The one-armed man was about forty-plus. He nodded. 'M-M-MacL-Lean,' he stammered. 'T-Tom MacL-Lean.'

Sam put a palm over his forehead. The man was burning up. 'You're feverish,' he said. 'You got a home I can take you to? Kin?'

'N-no sir . . . J-Just the b-b-back alleys . . . '

'I'd better get you back to my office an' out of those wet clothes, then,' Sam decided. After that he'd go scare up a doctor.

He helped MacLean to his feet. The

one-time blasting-engineer had to rest up against the wall until he got his breath back. Sam saw that he was short and malnourished, with wispy gray hair poking out from beneath his shabby hat.

'You think you can make it?' Sam asked him dubiously.

MacLean nodded. 'I'll t-t-try.' He looked up into Sam's long, shadowed face. 'You s-sure b-bein' kind to a st-stranger,' he husked.

'It's my job.'

A wave of nausea, or maybe giddiness, made MacLean bend forward at the waist, and fearing that he might collapse again, Sam went forward with him, reaching out to support him.

It was in that moment that a bullet plucked the air where he'd just been standing.

A moment later the crack of the gunshot tore across the sounds of merriment coming from the saloons further back up the street. Sam loosed a grunt of surprise. MacLean, retching, gave no indication that he even knew what was going on.

As Sam spun towards the rear of the darkened alley — the direction from which the shot had come — his right hand blurred towards the .44 at his hip.

Another shot crashed along the thoroughfare. It sounded high and sharp; whoever was out there was using a handgun, then. Sam dove to one side and hit the puddled ground with a splash and a curse.

The third shot came as he rolled and came back up onto his knees. At last MacLean began to wake up to the danger confronting them. 'Huh? Wh-wh-what — ?'

For one awful instant the mud tried to hold Sam down. Then he was up again, and the Remington was in his fist and stabbing at the darkness with three bright orange flashes, one after the other.

For a moment the alleyway was filled with noise. MacLean moaned and brought his one good arm up over his head to muffle the gunfire. Sam, paying him no mind, stepped quickly away from his muzzle-flashes, hunkered down and waited.

There was a pause of one heartbeat. Two, three, four —

As soon as his would-be assailant fired again, Sam was ready. Snap-aiming at the other man's muzzle-flash, he fired his remaining three shells with care, one straight at the flash and one to either side.

There was no cry or scream, just the sound of someone falling over a stack of cartons, then silence.

'W-w-what — ?'

'Shuddup, an' stay down.'

Without taking his eyes off the other end of the alley, Sam reloaded by feel. When he had six fresh shells in the handgun he rose and made his way down the alley, keeping his back to the right-side wall, ready to hit the mud at the first sign of trouble.

He was about sixty feet down the thoroughfare before he saw the body. It was sprawled facedown in the mud, arms splayed. A Colt's .45 was still clutched in the corpse's right hand.

Sam knew who it was even before he turned the dead man over. He just didn't know whether the sonofabitch'd been acting on his own initiative in an attempt to get even, or under orders. *Stover* orders.

He turned the corpse over.

Jess Coltrain's glassy blue eyes stared up into the dark night sky, unseeing.

8

Out on the near-black trail the steady beating of horse-hooves drew nearer. Belly-down behind the rocks off to the right, Matt and Harrigan strained to hear any sounds that might identify the riders.

Harrigan said, 'Do you — '

'Not so loud!'

'All right, all right. I was just gonna ask . . . do you think there's any chance it's *not* Baker an' his men out there?'

Matt threw a quick look at Harrigan's moon-washed face. The Irishman looked sick with worry. He nodded. 'There's always a chance. But who else would be ridin' this trail so late at night?'

Harrigan eyed him keenly through the gloom. 'How far away would you say they are?'

Matt shrugged. His voice was a taut

whisper. 'Hard to say. Sound travels on still nights like this. Maybe — ' He broke off suddenly, listening.

Harrigan heard it too. 'Voices!'

They held their breath, straining to pick out the fragments of low conversation now drifting towards them.

'Should . . . easy.'

'Don't bet on it.'

' . . . ber now . . . an' Andrews go to the north an' east, Taylor an' Miles to the . . . an' west . . . don't let 'em . . . 're there. Me an' Davis'll . . . 'em from behind when the time's right. You just . . . our lead.'

Again Matt and Harrigan exchanged looks. There was only one way they could take a conversation like that, and they took it. Harrigan licked his lips and tightened his grip on the Winchester in his clammy hands. Matt, beside him, reached forward to dab some spit on his own long-gun's foresight, to make it show up better in the darkness.

The thudding horse-hooves came ever nearer, mingling now with the faint jingle of harness and creak of leather.

Beside Matt, Harrigan tensed, but Matt had already picked them out; six riders bunched together with Johnny Baker in the lead. They were perhaps a hundred and twenty feet away, each of them etched with pale moonlight. The two watchers saw hunched shoulders, broad-brimmed hats pulled low. A couple of the riders, Baker included, held rifles at the ready.

They were following the ruts left in the sand by the two supply-wagons.

Suddenly one of the hard cases spoke. 'When should we split up?'

'Soon.'

'I just wouldn't want 'em to get too far ahead of us.'

'Don't worry, they won't.'

By now the riders were no more than thirty feet from the rocks. Matt sucked in a deep breath. The night air was pleasantly warm, and smelled of the greenery around them. Jacking a shell into his Winchester, he yelled, '*Hold it!*'

He sensed rather than saw their

surprise. And in the next few seconds he became aware of so much more; of the riders' muttered oaths and curses, the sudden, dangerous stiffening of their postures, the instinctive reaching for guns —

'*Hold it, I said!*' Matt repeated in a roar. '*Throw down your weapons an' there'll be no shootin'!*'

But Baker and co. had no intention of holding it, and even less of surrendering. It was plain enough to see what had happened. Their crafty little plan had been rumbled. But they were damned if they'd add insult to injury by giving up without a fight.

Johnny Baker brought his .44/40 around and fired a covering shot in the direction from which Matt's voice had come. Behind him three of his men hauled their horses around in a tight half-circle, preparing to retreat. The other two, whom Baker himself had identified as Davies and Andrews, followed Baker's lead and started shooting.

Matt slapped the stock of his Winchester to his cheek, sighted and fired. His first shot missed but his second slammed Davies out of the saddle and onto the ground, where he rolled around beneath the horse's hooves, clutching a wound high up on his right breast.

Baker fired another shot. It hit the rock just in front of Harrigan and exploded chips of stone into the Irishman's face.

As Harrigan leapt backwards, dropping his gun to claw at his eyes, Baker yelled something over his shoulder at the men who were about to flee, telling them to stand and fight. Matt triggered a third shot that made Baker shut up and duck low behind his horse's flying mane.

The night was trembling to gun blasts and yelling now. The spooked horses side-stepped and nickered in panic. Down on the ground Davies begged for help in a voice that was growing increasingly weak. Matt pumped another shell into his Winchester, brought the long-gun up on the bearded man called Miles, who was now emptying his Colt into the rocks, and fired.

The shot went higher than intended, drilling through Miles' head, and he spilled off his horse to land lifeless in the dust.

Harrigan stumbled back to the rocks. Matt tore his attention away from the fight just long enough to see his bloody face and watery eyes.

'You all right?'

Harrigan nodded, then said, 'Looks worse'n it is.'

He brought his long-gun up and fired half a dozen shots in quick succession. He didn't hit a thing, but he bought Matt enough time to take careful aim on Johnny Baker.

Because Baker was yelling again. The nostrils of his hooked nose were flared above his open mouth. He kept telling his men to stand and fight and kill the bastards in the rocks, that they were only a kid and a skinny little mick —

Matt figured he'd heard enough. He squeezed the trigger again and his Winchester boomed and bucked a little to one side. As he levered a fresh shell into the weapon, he saw Baker twitch up there on his prancing horse, and drop his rifle in order to grab his right shoulder.

For a moment Matt thought he was going to fall, but somehow he kept in the saddle, yelling, *'Get them! Get them!'* in a scratchy voice.

'The hell you say,' Matt replied in a low mutter.

He brought the Winchester up on Baker again just as the other man clawed for the Merwin & Hulbert high on his left hip. As the weapon cleared leather Matt squeezed the trigger and Baker fairly somersaulted off his horse in a crimson shower. This time Matt knew he was as dead as driftwood.

Beside him, Harrigan kept pouring lead out onto the trail until he was firing on empty. He still hadn't hit a thing, but with three out of the six Stover men down, he didn't need to. They'd made their point.

Baker's horse trampled heavily across Davies, who was now too dead to feel it. Taylor, a hard case with a handlebar moustache adorning his hare lip, paused to fire one final shot. Harrigan, tossing his empty Winchester aside, grabbed Matt's left-side Tranter from its holster, brought it up and fired back, twice.

Taylor reached for his Adam's apple and gave a weird, keening scream that they all heard above the other sounds of battle. Then he went limp and toppled from his saddle.

After that it was pretty much all over. Andrews and his nameless partner spun their horses around and galloped off back the way they'd come. Four now-riderless mounts followed them at a hard run.

Moonlight shafted down across the trail, illuminating the bodies they'd left behind them. Matt waited a while, then stood up. As Harrigan watched, he went out onto the rutted road to check each one in turn. When he was sure they were all dead, he hauled them over to the side of the trail.

Harrigan was shivering, and his thin face was bloody from the lacerated skin up around his eyes, where the rock chips had struck him. 'Will they be back?' he asked, stepping out into the open with the Tranter still held in his right hand. He seemed to have trouble getting the words around the lump in his throat.

Matt shrugged, none too steady himself now that it was all over. 'I doubt it,' he replied, going over to their picketed horses. 'We did better'n I thought, gettin' four out of six of 'em. But you never can tell.' He watched the Irishman reclaim his discarded long-gun. 'We'll keep a close eye on our back-trail,' he decided at length. 'Just in case.'

★ ★ ★

Kate Stover's voice was as cool as iced water.

'So,' she said calmly. 'It is as we feared.'

Dale, seated across from her in the sun-filled parlor, nodded grimly. His cruelly handsome face was tight with anger, and his mother couldn't really say that she blamed him.

'Yes,' he replied after a while. 'It's as we *expected*. Ever since that sono-fabuck Judge came in and closed me down last week, our takings at the *Pot of Gold* have dropped by almost seventy-five per cent. Nobody wants to drink there anymore. Nobody wants to *gamble* there anymore. The place is like a morgue most nights. And that's not *all*.'

Gene, who'd been standing over by the open window, turned around sharply. His thin, sickly face was dotted with shadows cast by sun through lace. 'There's more?' he wheezed.

'Oh, there's more, all right. Three merchants have refused to pay us our concession this week. That's right; just flat-out *refused*. Ever since Judge killed Jess Coltrain last Thursday night, it seems these storekeepers have grown balls — if you'll excuse my language, Mother.'

Kate gestured absently with one small hand.

'Everything was running smoothly until he came along. Now he's doing everything he can to undermine our authority,' Dale went on venomously. 'He's shown this rabble that we can be defied; and the sooner he pays for that, the better I'll like it.'

'We tried to make him pay last *week*,' Gene pointed out, coming over to perch on the edge of his mother's chair. 'And what did we get for our troubles? Jess Coltrain was a good man, maybe our best. If anyone should've been able to deal with Judge, it was him.'

Dale eyed his brother sidelong. 'What are you saying, then? That we've met our match?'

'Of course not — '

'No, I should hope not! We've never yet come across the lawman we couldn't buy or bury.'

'No,' said Kate, getting to her feet and brushing imaginary creases from the front of her peach-colored cotton dress. 'But there's a first time for everything, Dale.'

'Mother?'

She went over to the mantelpiece and ran her fingers along the polished mahogany in search of dust. She knew her sons were watching her expectantly, she saw their puzzled, angry faces in the reflection of the gilt-edged mirror hanging over the fireplace.

'I've been thinking,' she said softly. 'All the problems Judge has caused us . . . Perhaps we should consider moving on.'

'*What?*' Dale came out of his chair fast, eyeing her in disbelief. 'You're not serious! Admit defeat? Allow that glorified old dinosaur the satisfaction of knowing he's *beaten* us — '

She turned around to face them

both. 'That glorified old dinosaur,' she snapped, 'is considerably younger than me.'

Dale's eyes dropped. 'I'm sorry. I didn't mean — '

'I know you didn't. But there's a lot to be said for age,' she said. 'The longer you live, the more you learn. And unless I'm much mistaken, our Marshal Judge has learned quite a bit in his time.'

Something in Kate's voice made Dale look at her more closely. A frown lowered his eyebrows, for he'd never heard his mother talk in quite that way about any man, not even his father. 'It couldn't be,' he said bluntly, 'that your interest in that old man goes beyond the professional, could it?'

Her face registered the offence she felt, and she had to fight the impulse to strike him. 'No, it couldn't,' she replied in a low, strong voice. 'But I've already lost one son here in King Creek. I have no wish to lose more.'

There was a knock at the door. Dale studied his mother a moment longer,

217

then turned and crossed the room to answer it. He felt angry at his own jealousy, but unable to contain it. He opened the door and found one of their hired men, Faver, standing out in the hallway. 'Yes?'

Half a minute later he closed the door again and turned to face his mother and brother. He looked tired and irritable.

'Dale? Dale, what is it?'

Ignoring his brother, Dale went over to the drinks tray and poured himself a healthy measure of whiskey. Without turning around to face them he said, 'Dick Whiteley's outside. He brought us some news. Walt Sullivan's supply-wagons have just entered town.'

For a moment neither Kate nor Gene asked the question they wanted answering. At last Gene said, 'Johnny Baker . . . ?'

'Nowhere to be seen.' Dale turned around so fast that some of the whiskey slopped over the rim of his glass and splashed onto the Oriental rug at his feet. 'But right up alongside the wagons, Judge's deputy and Randolph's murderer, as large as life and twice as healthy!'

Kate closed her eyes, feeling quite weak. So . . . She had no option but to accept the truth; that Baker and his men had failed in their attempt to take control of Walt Sullivan's supplies — and presumably paid the price for that failure.

'That clinches it, then,' said Gene, coughing into his handkerchief. 'Something's got to be done about Judge — fast.'

Dale nodded. 'I agree. Mother?'

Kate's eyes snapped open. 'Would it do any good to tell you what I think?' she asked sardonically.

Gene came to his feet and reached out with one thin hand. 'You shouldn't worry for me, Mother. We have eight men to back us. Judge is just one man. His only ally is a boy.'

'A boy who fought off Johnny Baker and his men to bring those wagons through in one piece.'

Dale set his glass down. 'Mother . . . I appreciate your concern. We both do. But surely you can see that moving on is no answer. If we up stakes now, that's it. Our reputation is shot to pieces. We must show strength and unity . . . whip those fools down there back into line — '

'And how do you propose to do that? By making another attempt on Judge's life?' Kate went over and put a hand on Dale's arm. 'Don't you understand? You can't win *either* way, not any more. If you kill Judge now, you turn him into a martyr.'

'And if we let him live,' Gene husked, 'six merchants will refuse to pay next week's concession, and nine the week after.'

'Gene's right,' said Dale, disengaging himself from his mother. 'But, in your own way, so are you.'

'Then what is the answer?'

Dale gave the matter some quick thought. 'I'm not sure. Yet. But there *must* be some way to get him off our backs without turning him into a champion of the people — and so help me, I'm going to find it.'

★   ★   ★

'Hey, marshal — you wouldn't happen to have any of that coffee goin' spare, would you?'

Sam looked up from the fire-blackened range, where he'd been pouring himself a mug of Arbuckle's and pondering the problems of King Creek. As soon as his mild gray eyes lit upon the two figures standing in the open doorway a rare smile cracked his lips.

'Matt! By God, boy . . . You fellers just got in?'

Matt and Harrigan came into the office and while Harrigan closed the door behind them, Sam came forward to clap his son on the arm, more relieved to see them both than he could've imagined.

'Yessir, just got in an' left Sullivan droolin' over his supplies.'

'Have any trouble?'

'Some.' Matt took off his hat and threw it onto the sofa. While Sam filled two more mugs with coffee, he briefly recounted their shoot-out with Baker and his plug-uglies. 'We didn't relish the killin' of four men,' he concluded, 'but we had precious few problems with the return trip once our guns had done their talkin'.'

'Well, I sure am glad to see you-all back in one piece. You too, Harrigan.'

'What's it been like here in town these last couple o' weeks?'

Sam, now seated behind the desk with Mitzi curled up on his lap, told them about closing down the *Pot of Gold*, and Jess Coltrain's attempt on his life. 'Apart from that, things've been real quiet. Pearl's still bearin' up, an' Jack's lookin' better every day, though he still can't get the hang of usin' crutches.'

Matt indicated the open cell with a

nod. 'So who's your prisoner?'

Sam glanced around in surprise. He'd forgotten all about the figure now stirring on one of the cell-bunks, even though he'd been there for the past five days. 'Oh, that's MacLean. He's not a prisoner, just a feller who's had the grippe an' nowhere to rest up 'till it passes.'

On the bunk, Tom MacLean was struggling to sit up and eye the newcomers. Ever since Sam had brought him back to the office that rainy night, dried him off and fetched him a doctor to take a look at him, he'd spent most of his time sleeping. It was one way to pass the giddy hours while his touch of 'flu ran its course. But he'd been getting steadily stronger these last two days, and some clearer in the head, though his craving for *Vin Vitae* sometimes made him wander. Still, the marshal had looked after him good, though he'd doubtless never admit it, and MacLean, who didn't run into kindness all that often, was beholden.

223

'You, ah, you made any progress findin' out who *really* killed Randolph Stover?' Harrigan asked uneasily. Out on the trail, with other problems to occupy him, it had been easy to forget that there was a murder charge hanging over his head. Last night and this morning, however, the knowledge had come back to haunt him with a vengeance.

His heart sank when Sam shook his graying head. 'Not a bit,' he confessed. 'An' it galls me somethin' fierce to admit it, believe me. If I could just figure out *why* the sonofabitch was murdered, I could probably get a handle on the thing, but as it is, all we know for sure is that he had his face caved in by a heavy-caliber shell fired from the alley directly opposite the store.'

Harrigan wrung his hands in despair, 'Where does that leave me, then? You can only hold them Stovers off for so long, you know. After that they'll be wantin' my head on a plate.'

'M-m-marshal?'

Sam swiveled around to face the one-armed blasting-engineer, who was now sitting up on the edge of his bunk, running his hand across his tired, weasel's face. 'You got a problem, MacLean?'

'A h-heavy-c-caliber shell,' the little man repeated. 'You mean the kind that'd c-come from a r-rifle?'

'Yeah.'

MacLean squinted down at the floor, obviously trying to drag a hazy memory out of the mists clouding his brain. 'I s-s-saw someone . . . ' he said quietly. 'We r-run into each other the n-night of the k-killin'. In the alley right ac-cross from the st-store.' He looked up to find all three of them watching him keenly, and felt a sudden craving for *Vin Vitae* that nearly made him swoon. 'H-he wuz c-carryin' a rifle,' he finished, swallowing hard.

Sam set the cat down on the floor and stood up. 'You're sure it was the night of the killin'?' he asked carefully.

'Y-yessir. F-first I heard of it wuz the v-very next d-day, just after you had th-that r-run-in with Charlie C-Coyote.'

Sam glanced from Matt to Harrigan, then went across to lean up against the open cell door. 'Who was it?' he asked.

MacLean peered up at him through watery eyes. 'He g-give me five bucks,' he said. 'F-for no g-good reason.'

'Except maybe to shut you up,' said Harrigan.

'Who was it?' Sam asked again, feeling his belly-muscles beginning to clench in anticipation.

MacLean told them.

Sam let out a low breath. 'You're sure he was totin' a long-gun?'

'Y-yessir.'

'An' runnin' away from the store?'

'Y-yessir.'

Sam nodded, then turned around slowly, keeping his face neutral in case his excitement built Harrigan's hopes up. 'All right,' he said. 'Maybe we've got a new suspect, maybe we haven't. Either way, we won't know for sure until we brace 'im. Matt — you fit?'

'Uh-huh.'

Sam went over to the door and lifted his hat from the nail. 'Come on, then; let's ride.'

★ ★ ★

'You've done *what*?' Kate Stover stared aghast at her eldest surviving son and shook her head in disbelief. 'Are you totally mad?'

Dale bit off an angry response. His mother ought to know better than to undermine him in front of a hired man like Dick Whiteley. 'Half an hour ago I told you I'd find a way of dealing with Judge. Well, I found it. And implemented it.'

'Without consulting your brother and me?' Kate's bright brown eyes fairly burned into his face. 'My God, Dale. Whatever possessed you to — '

Dale shrugged, determined to weather the storm. 'Mother, I'll grant you that my plan is by no means perfect. But we have to do *something*. And what I've set into motion will deal with Judge far more effectively than any amount of words.'

She remained unconvinced. Tears moved in her eyes, but she refused to let them flow. 'Stop it,' she said. 'Call your men off.'

'I can't,' Dale replied. 'They left fifteen minutes ago.' His dark eyes shuttled toward the clock on the mantel. 'They're probably there by now.'

'Then may God help you,' she said in a whisper. 'Because Judge won't desist. He'll just become all the more determined.' Again she shook her head. 'Can't you see that you've signed your own death-warrant, Dale?'

'Excuse me, Miss Kate.'

Kate turned to face Dick Whiteley, who was turning his beaver hat nervously in his hands. 'I don't mean to speak out of turn, but I'd say what Dale's done is right. Judge himself doesn't know the meaning of fear. But for the safety of a loved one, or one he holds in high regard — '

'I'll thank you to keep your misguided opinions to yourself,' Kate told him acidly. Again she turned her hot gaze on Dale. 'At least *try* to call your men off before it's too late. For *my* sake, Dale. You won't accomplish a single thing by — '

'Well, well, well.' Gene turned away from the open window, where he'd been getting some fresh air in order to loosen the tightness in his chest. 'Speak of the devil.'

Dale frowned at him. 'What? What's that you said?'

'Judge,' Gene replied, pointing at the gently-shifting curtain beside him. 'And his deputy. Coming this way.'

Kate put a hand on Dale's arm. 'You see! He — '

'Whatever he's here for, it has nothing to do with the business we've just been discussing. It's too soon for that.'

'Well, what *does* he want?'

'How should I know? To gloat, perhaps? That Sullivan's supplies came through in one piece? That his looks and charm have made a woman old enough to know better run around like a headless chicken?'

Kate had heard enough. With fury sparkling in her eyes she lashed out, slapping Dale across the face with enough force to snap his head sideways.

Silence collapsed over the room, but for Gene's tortured breathing. Dale made no move whatsoever. His right cheek grew slowly red. A lifetime later he turned to face her again.

'I will never forgive you for that, Mother,' he said softly.

Before Kate could form a reply, the jangling of the bell-pull made all heads turn towards the parlor door.

Suddenly Kate felt nauseous. Somehow their whole way of life here in King Creek was turning sour. She swayed dangerously, listening to the distant exchange of words between the man assigned guard duty and the marshal.

Footsteps clattered across the hall-way. The guard said, 'Hey, you can't just walk in here — ' There was a smacking sound. Kate almost moaned when she heard a body thudding to the floor.

Then the parlor door opened and Judge and Dury came in.

The silence fairly *congealed*.

Sam touched the brim of his hat politely. 'Ma'am.' His gray eyes moved from one face to the other, the smallest of smiles playing across his lips.

Kate met his gaze only with effort. When he said no more she knew she would have to break the silence or go mad. She cleared her throat. 'Marshal. Might I ask the meaning of this . . . visit?'

He nodded. 'Sure.' Again his eyes travelled over them all before going back to Kate. 'It's about this trouble with Randolph.'

Kate felt her pulses quicken. 'Ran — you mean there's been some developments at last?'

'There's been a development, yes'm. Seems a feller was seen leggin' it away from the store on the night of the killin'. Feller totin' a rifle. Feller who paid the man who saw him five lousy dollars to keep his mouth shut.' Sam's expression turned to granite as he raised his left hand and singled one of them out. 'Vow,' he said quietly.

9

'Wh-what?'

All eyes turned to Dick Whiteley.

The former deputy looked dumb-struck. Even as they watched, the blood was sponged from his thick-featured face, making his short, tobacco-colored hair look even darker. Then he recovered himself sufficiently to speak. 'What the hell *is* this, Judge? What witness? For God's sake, man, I was *investigating* the case when you came along and forced me out of office!'

Sam appeared totally unmoved. 'We can do this the hard way or the easy way,' he replied. 'It's entirely up to you.'

'But . . . ' Whiteley looked from Dale to Gene, from Gene to Kate, from Kate to Matt, from Matt back to Sam. 'Hell-fire, man, I don't even *own* a rifle!'

Gene stepped forward. 'Hold on,

there! You own a Martini-Henry. I've seen it; it's a beautiful weapon.'

Whiteley's brown eyes bugged. '*That?* I . . . I sold it. 'Bout three months ago.'

Matt asked, 'Who'd you sell it to?'

'What? Uh . . . '

Sam had heard enough to convince him that they'd found the man they were after. He stepped forward slowly, so's not to spook the former deputy into doing anything rash. 'Give it up, Whiteley. You won't do yourself any favors by draggin' it out any longer.'

Whiteley instinctively took a step away from him. 'But I'm *innocent*, I tell you!'

Maybe he was, too, as doubtful as it seemed. But then he went and proved otherwise. One moment he was muttering and mumbling and backing away, presumably in fear; the next he was going for the New Line Police Colt in the holster beneath his right armpit.

Sam yelled, '*Down!*' and Kate screamed as he pushed her aside. Dale shouted something into all the confusion that he didn't catch. Whiteley's left hand came out from the folds of his too-tight gray town suit filled with iron; and then the sunny parlor was filled with gun blasts, and Kate screamed some more.

Whiteley caught the bullets from Matt's Tranter's right in his barrel chest and crashed back into the wall. As darker blood jumped from the wounds he fired one round into the floor, then hunched his shoulders. Dale was still shouting. So was Gene. Sam heard other Stover men thundering through the house, asking each other what was going on, and he yelled, 'Keep them out of here!'

Then Whiteley's legs went out from under him and he collapsed across the Oriental rug, his breath sawing in and out, in and out —

Sam flicked a glance at Matt. The younger man was still locked in a crouch, his twin Tranters still smoking slowly in his fists. Then he went over to the wounded man, and kneeling, turned him over.

'Whiteley? Can you hear me?'

The parlor door burst open and three men jammed into the frame with handguns drawn. Gene hurried over to them with his hands held palms-out. 'It's all right! Get back outside!'

On the floor, Whiteley stared up at Sam through pain-glazed eyes. Blood stained his teeth; a thin worm of it was sliding down his square chin. He was weeping.

'Why'd you do it, Dick?' Sam asked quietly. The dying man didn't hear him at first, so Sam asked him again.

'Why?' The one-time deputy's voice was cracked and gurgly. 'I'll tell you . . . why.' His moist brown eyes moved over to Kate. 'Because of *her*.'

Kate brought one hand up to her mouth. '*Me*?'

'Yeah . . . you. Because I was sick and tired of being . . . just another hired hand. Because I wanted to . . . get closer to you. To be something . . . *more* to you . . . given time, your husband, perhaps.'

Whiteley sobbed some more, his tears mixing with the blood he was choking up. 'But I made a . . . mistake,' he continued. 'Poor be . . . besotted fool that I was. 'Stead of biding my . . . time . . . keeping my own counsel . . . I told Randolph how much I . . . admired you, Miss Kate . . . and he . . . he wasted little time in warning me off.' His eyes cleared a little. 'You know . . . he called himself your s . . . son . . . but if you ask me, he behaved more like . . . your *guardian*.'

'So you killed him,' Matt said, coming over.

Whiteley nodded sluggishly. 'Knew I'd never get anywhere while he . . . stood in my way,' he said. 'He . . . had too much influence over you, Kate . . . hell, you never made a . . . a move without consulting him . . . first.'

Sam shook his head. 'You crazy — ' But then he fell silent, realizing that Whiteley was beyond hearing him. He reached down and closed the dead man's sightless eyes.

★   ★   ★

Kate was understandably shaken up. Gene too. But Dale was a hard one, and he took charge of everything. Within fifteen minutes he had the body wrapped in a sheet and stretched out on the veranda to await collection by the local undertaker, whom Sam had promised to send back up, and two of his hired gunnies hard at work cleaning up the parlor.

Knowing they'd serve no useful purpose by hanging around any longer, Sam and Matt decided to leave them to it. It was as they were mounting up out front that Kate appeared in the column-flanked doorway, carefully keeping her eyes off the sheet-wrapped corpse to her right.

'Marshal!'

Sam settled himself comfortably aboard his roan and looked up at her expectantly. 'Yes, ma'am?'

238

Something in her expression suggested more trouble than that which she'd already experienced, and his lawman's instincts made him frown. She opened her mouth but nothing came out. It was as if she was trying to decide what to do for the best.

Then Dale appeared behind her, placed a hand on her shoulder. She jumped. 'We just want you to know, marshal,' he said smoothly. 'We're grateful for what you did here today — but it doesn't change a thing.'

Sam eyed him levelly. 'Didn't think for one moment that it would.'

'Good. I daresay we'll be locking horns again then. Soon.'

Again Sam's instincts sent out a warning tingle. He held Dale's gaze for a moment longer, wondering what the sonofabitch was trying to imply, then said, 'Who knows? Maybe next time we'll be playin' for keeps.'

'Oh, we will,' Dale replied with a humorless smile. 'We will.'

Sam swapped a curious look with

Matt, then the two of them swung their horses around and started back toward town at a canter.

Dale, following their progress, felt his mother's eyes burn into him. 'You fool,' she whispered harshly. 'You know what you've done by instigating this scheme of yours, don't you? You've declared open war.'

Her son smiled down at her. 'You'll be singing a different tune by the end of the day,' he promised, touching his cheek where she'd slapped him. 'Because I guarantee that Judge will be dead and buried by sundown.'

* * *

They stopped off at the undertaker's tent and Sam told the mortician that he had a body to collect up at the Stover place.

'Dale?' the mortician asked eagerly. 'Gene?'

'Dick Whiteley.'

Some of the fire left the other man's

eyes. 'Ah well, can't complain, I guess. I been lookin' forward to embalmin' *that* sonuver, too.'

The King Creek lawmen remounted and headed on back to their office. As soon as they walked through the door Pat Harrigan said, 'Marshal Judge — thank God!'

Sam was on the alert at once. Coming further into the room he saw Jack Denton sprawled out on the horsehair sofa, two crutches propped up against the wall nearby, and felt a sudden stab of foreboding. '*Jack?*'

He pushed past Harrigan and went over to the former marshal. Denton's lumpy, square-jawed face was pale and haunted. Dried tear-streaks smudged his stubble-shaded cheeks, and his lips looked puffy and bruised. 'Judge, for God's sake — '

'What is it? What's happened?'

'Pearl! The bastards, they've taken her!'

Matt came over. '*Who's* taken her?'

Denton shook his head to clear it. He

felt jumpy, confused and frustrated. 'Stover's men. Faver was one of 'em, Burden the other . . . '

'Evidently they turned up at Denton's place about an hour ago,' said Harrigan. 'Just forced their way in, beat Denton around a little, snatched Pearl away and left him with a message — for you.'

Sam's teeth clenched. In the corner Mitzi watched him through worried sea-green eyes. 'I can guess the gist of it, but tell me anyway,' he said tensely.

Denton himself supplied the answer. 'They want you to resign your post and get out of town by four o'clock today, or else . . . or else — '

Sam raised a hand to stop him. 'All right, Jack, all right.' He watched the other man bury his head in his hands. 'So long as we go, you'll get Pearl back safely.'

'An' just to make sure we don't come *back*,' Matt added grimly, 'they'll escort us out of town — an' then shoot us.'

'I doubt they'll wait that long,' said

Denton, regaining some of his composure. 'You . . . you're to stop in at the *Pot of Gold* before you leave town.'

'For good old Dale to say fare thee well, eh?' Sam nodded with deadly calm, and drew his Remington from leather. 'Harrigan, go fetch me that scattergun from the rifle-rack.'

Matt studied his profile. 'What you got in mind, Sam?'

Sam glanced up from checking the handgun's loads. 'A little slice of good, old-fashioned justice,' he replied steadily. 'I've suffered them Stovers for long enough. This time they've gone too far. I aim to make sure they don't do it again. *Ever.*'

Matt nodded his understanding. 'Sounds good,' he said. 'Count me in.'

Harrigan came back from the rifle-rack. 'Me too,' he added quietly.

Sam looked from one to the other, then took hold of the Greener shotgun. 'All right.' And that was when the law office doors swung open and they all got the shock of their lives.

It was four o'clock in the afternoon and the *Pot of Gold* was like a tomb. The lone barkeeper — Dale had been forced to let the other two go — was polishing glasses with a damp towel and trying hard to ignore the tension in the big room. He wasn't finding it easy.

Four men were sitting at the far end of the bar: Faver, Burden, Peters and Jones. Another three — Sawyer, Cousins and O'Leary — were playing five-card stud for matches at one of the corner tables. Easton, the eighth man, was spinning one of the roulette wheels over and over again, watching the numbers blur around just to kill time.

The barkeeper, whose name was Bradley, finished the glass he was working on and threw the damp towel under the counter. He'd guessed that something was up the minute Faver and Burden had brought that fat woman into the place just over an hour earlier.

She'd struggled like hell, he remembered, kicked and spat and swore like a veteran. Then Faver had punched her. Bradley hadn't liked that, but he'd known better than to say as much.

While the fat woman was dazed they'd dragged her upstairs. Pretty soon the rest of the Stover hard cases had filtered in, each of them loaded for bear. About half an hour later Dale and Gene had put in an appearance. Neither of them had said much, just hurried straight upstairs themselves.

Time had passed. Then Faver, who'd been standing watch on the woman, came down to join his companions. He'd switched on the Pianola and started humming along to the tinny melody it gave out.

Then they'd all started waiting.

A thick-bearded miner, hearing the music, had pushed expectantly through the batwings. Easton had looked up from the roulette wheel and said, 'Beat it — we're not open.'

Ten taut minutes later Bradley finally

decided he'd had enough. He was there to dispense cheer, not become party to whatever dirty scheme the Stovers were hatching now.

He took off his apron and grabbed his jacket. Shrugging into it, he came around the bar and started across the floor on shaky legs. He was halfway to the batwings when Faver asked him where in hell he thought he was going.

'Anywhere,' he replied over his shoulder, 'so long as it's nowhere near *this* place.'

He pushed through the batwings and out onto the street, almost bumping into someone coming along the boardwalk. 'Uh . . . 'scuse me.'

Sam Judge said, 'Sure.'

Bradley looked up at him. Suddenly everything made sense. As he hustled away from the saloon, Sam paused a moment. He glanced around and asked his companions if they were ready. They said they were.

He pushed through the batwings and walked into the saloon, Matt and

Harrigan behind him.

Their sudden appearance sent a stiffening ripple through the men at the bar and at the corner table. Sam, coming to a halt in the centre of the big room, brought the Greener shotgun up and said, 'All right — where is she?'

Faver's black eyes shifted from the shotgun's barrels to Sam's long face. He hadn't forgotten the pain he'd suffered the day Sam had batted him in the face with his own rifle. 'The fat woman, you mean?' He smiled. 'She's safe. Got a few extra lumps'n she had before, but safe.' He turned to the man standing next to him, Peters. 'Go tell Dale his friends've arrived.'

Peters moved away from the bar, his boots clattering against the sawdust-covered boards and his sunburst spurs jingling musically. Sam kept his eyes on Faver, knowing that either Matt or Harrigan would make sure Peters did nothing more than he'd been told.

A minute later they heard footsteps hurrying back along the corridor upstairs. Then Peters reappeared with Dale and Gene beside him. Sam immediately noticed that Dale was wearing a black leather gunbelt. Gene a similar rig holding a Peacemaker. They got as far as the gallery rail, then came to a halt, giving themselves a height advantage. Gene was looking almighty nervous, Dale supremely confident. Not surprisingly, it was Dale who did all the talking.

'I told you we'd be locking horns again soon, didn't I, Judge?'

Sam nodded. 'An' I told you that next time we'd be playin' for keeps.'

'Denton outlined the terms?'

'Uh-huh. I'm to resign as town marshal an' get the hell out of town. Well . . .' With his free hand he reached up and pulled the shield from his jacket, tossing it onto one of the roulette tables. 'There's my resignation. I'll be movin' along just as soon as you release Pearl.'

Dale's smile widened. The sonofa-bitch looked as if he was actually enjoying himself. 'I'll thank you to give up your weapons first. All of you.'

Sam shook his head. 'You can go to hell with that request,' he said, snorting. 'Now release the woman, Stover, or so help me I'll — '

'You'll *what?*' Slowly Dale came down four of the steps. 'You're in no position to do *anything*, Judge. Oh, you had a good run for your money, I'll grant you that. But *I'm* holding all the aces now.'

Sam said, 'Maybe you are. But I don't *need* any aces. I've got two jacks to back my play. Two jacks an' a queen.'

Dale eyed him sharply, suddenly alert. Up on the gallery Gene muttered, '*What?*'

Behind Sam the batwings creaked open and a fourth figure stepped inside. Kate Stover came to a halt beside Sam, staring up at her sons through moist, tortured eyes.

Gene said, '*Mother!*'

But Dale wasn't so much surprised as furious. 'What in the name of God do you think *you're* doing here?'

'I'm trying to stop this wretched business before it goes any further,' Kate replied in a voice thick with emotion.

Dale regarded her with contempt. 'You mean you've *willingly* taken sides against us?'

Kate said, 'It's not a case of taking sides. Our normal business dealings here in King Creek are one thing, but *this* madness is something else. It's gone far enough, Dale, and it can only end one way. So release the woman, now. *Please!*'

Dale shook his head, his eyes shining brightly. 'You're wrong, Mother,' he said venomously. 'This 'madness', as you call it, hasn't gone nearly far *enough!*'

Even before the last word left his lips he went for the Smith & Wesson American at his hip, and Gene, fearing for his mother's safety, yelled, '*Dale, no!*'

Suddenly the rest of his men were

taking that as their cue to haul iron, and Harrigan was lunging forward to knock the woman to the floor, where her chances of stopping a stray bullet would be considerably lessened.

Easton, the man nearest to Sam, went for his butt-forward Cavalry Colt. Spotting the move, Sam spun towards him and fired the Greener.

The shotgun charge practically tore Easton apart. As he flew backwards across one of the roulette tables, Sam swung the riot gun around in a smooth arc that brought it up to line on Faver, Burden and Jones, who were still bunched together at the bar.

Faver bawled, '*Get him, quick!*'

But they weren't going to be quick enough. The shotgun roared again, shredding Jones worst of all and peppering Faver and Burden bad enough to send them scampering for cover.

Within seconds the saloon was transformed into a battleground. Matt crabbed sideways to get behind the meager cover of a roulette table, firing both Tranters as he went. Harrigan, crouching over the struggling woman like a human shield, used his borrowed Winchester to keep Peters from shooting down at them from the gallery above. In the middle of the room, Sam switched the now-empty shotgun from his right hand to his left and drew his .44, determined to put as many of his enemies down as he could.

Kate screamed, 'For *God's sake . . . Please — stop it!*'

Above them, Gene rushed to the head of the stairs and said, 'Dale, call them off!'

The hard case called Burden got off three shots that dug gashes into the baize of the roulette table before Matt came back out from behind it and plugged him twice in the chest. More lead whined through the air, thudding into tables, the bar top and the still-playing Pianola. One of the overhead oil-lamps shattered, spilling kerosene everywhere. Harrigan suddenly screamed and fell away from Kate, clutching a ruined shoulder.

Again Gene begged Dale to call their men off. 'For God's sake, that's our mother down there!'

Dale, crouching on the staircase and firing through the balusters, threw him a look that Gene had never seen before. With his free hand he touched the cheek Kate had slapped earlier. '*Whose* mother?' he asked.

The saloon stank of blood. Shattered bottles added a sickly-sweet stench of moonshine to the odor. Sam felt a bullet sing past his ear.

Triggering one more shot in return, he dove for the nearest cover, the Pianola. While Matt kept up covering fire and Harrigan fought to hold Kate Stover down and nurse his shoulder-wound at the same time, Sam broke open the Greener and pulled fresh shells from his jacket pocket.

Faver came up from behind the bar. His left arm was stinging like a bitch where the second charge of buckshot had caught it. He leveled his S&W Russian at the plainest target — Harrigan — and was just about to squeeze the trigger when Matt came out from behind the roulette table again and shot him twice in the head.

Above the din Gene said, 'All right, all right, that's enough! Hold your fire!'

Dale's eyes snapped in his direction. 'What the hell are you playing at?'

'That's our mother down there! What if she's already been — '

Dale said, 'Tough.' And shot him.

Gene cried out and grabbed his stomach, then fell onto his back, writhing. At once Kate renewed her screams, and the attention of the Stover men became divided between the fight at ground level and events taking place upstairs.

Dale yelled down, 'Well, what are you waiting for? *Kill them!*'

And that was when Sam came out from behind the Pianola with the reloaded shotgun in his hands, crossed the room at a run, came to a halt at the foot of the stairs and let go both barrels in Dale's direction.

The result was devastating. As Dale's mouth opened wide in a scream, his gray vest suddenly burst apart, exposing red meat where his chest had been a moment before. The buckshot threw him against the wall, and when he bounced off he left an ugly red smear behind him. He fell forward and came head over heels down the stairs, his gun falling from his hand.

He rolled to a stop at Sam's feet, eyes bulging, mouth wide, teeth bloody. His chest looked like something a butcher might have tenderized.

The Pianola stopped playing at last.

The sound that replaced it was Kate's uncontrollable sobbing.

Sam turned to face the surviving gunmen, who were beginning to come out from behind cover in order to stare down at their employer's corpse. He felt tired and scratchy as he said, 'It's over. Understand me? The gravy-train's finished its run, boys — so get the hell out of town, or so help me I'll arrest you all!'

Then he threw the shotgun aside and went upstairs to find Pearl.

★ ★ ★

'We're beholden to you, Judge. *Real* beholden.'

Sam released his grip on Jack Denton's right hand and said, 'Forget it. But if ever you should need a hand around here again . . . '

'Thanks. But something tells me life in King Creek'll be considerably quieter now that Kate Stover's gone back home to Wisconsin.' Denton looked around the office — *his* office again, now that he'd mastered the use of his crutches and hired himself a deputy by the name of Harrigan and a one-armed turnkey called MacLean. 'You know, she was damned lucky she didn't lose that youngest boy of hers. Gut-shot like he was . . . there's not many that pull through.'

'I suspicion that's why she decided to quit the vulturin' game once an' for all,' said Matt, who was standing beside his older partner with his hat in his hands. 'She didn't want to push that luck an' risk losin' anythin' else.'

'You could have a point there, boy.' Denton got to his feet, settled his crutches into his armpits and propelled himself around the desk. 'Well, just make sure you remember, you'll be welcome here *anytime*, the pair of you.'

'And that goes double for me,' said Pearl, stepping forward to give them each a rib-cracking hug. 'So long, Matt. Look after this old reprobate here for me, will you?'

'I'll surely do that, ma'am,' Matt replied, clapping his hat down on his head.

Pearl embraced Sam, said quietly, 'Take care of yourself, Sam.'

He kissed her lightly on the forehead. 'I always do.' Then he held her at arm's length, gave her a wink and said, 'So long, Pearl.'

There was a curious ring of finality to the words, as if he were really saying farewell to what might have been a decade earlier.

They went out onto the boardwalk, and while Matt stepped up to leather, Sam bent down, scooped Mitzi into his left hand and deposited her none too gently inside one of his saddlebags. By the time he had also climbed into the saddle, the fat Abyssinian cat had stuck her head out of the pouch and was eyeing the Dentons sleepily.

Judge and Dury touched their fingers to their hat-brims, backed their horses away from the hitch-rack and pointed them on a course that would take them back along Main Street and out of town on the same road that had brought them there in the first place.

Their work in King Creek, Nevada, was done. But a few months from now there would be fresh adventures to occupy them; adventures that involved the U.S. Army, a bunch of renegade Apaches and a lost little girl a thousand miles from home.

But hell, that's another story — and one of these days it will doubtless be told.

We do hope that you have enjoyed reading this large print book.

Did you know that all of our titles are available for purchase?

We publish a wide range of high quality large print books including:
**Romances, Mysteries, Classics
General Fiction
Non Fiction and Westerns**

Special interest titles available in large print are:
**The Little Oxford Dictionary
Music Book, Song Book
Hymn Book, Service Book**

Also available from us courtesy of Oxford University Press:
**Young Readers' Dictionary
(large print edition)
Young Readers' Thesaurus
(large print edition)**

For further information or a free brochure, please contact us at:
**Ulverscroft Large Print Books Ltd.,
The Green, Bradgate Road, Anstey,
Leicester, LE7 7FU, England.
Tel:** (00 44) **0116 236 4325
Fax:** (00 44) **0116 234 0205**

QUICK ON THE DRAW

Steve Hayes

Luke Chance has one claim to fame: he's real quick on the draw. Trying to outrun a reputation he doesn't want, he ends up in Rattlesnake Springs — where he meets the beautiful Teddy Austin. Teddy hires him to break horses on her father's ranch, but pretty soon Luke is locking horns with the Shadow Hills foreman, Thad McClory. As if that wasn't enough, the Austins are also having trouble with their neighbors. Though he doesn't want to get involved, it seems Luke can't help but do so . . .

COLTER'S QUEST

Neil Hunter

1622: An expedition of Spanish soldiers, carrying a hoard of gold and silver, loses its way in the mountains. Now the last man alive, Father Ignacio Corozon, hides the treasure in a cave . . . 1842: Josiah Colter stumbles across that very same cave and discovers the cache . . . 1888: Josiah's grandson Ben has his home burned to the ground, his wife kidnapped, and his friend killed. Chet Ballard and Jess McCall set out alongside him to find Rachel and avenge the murder . . .

THE KILLING OF JERICHO SLADE

Paxton Johns

When Jericho Slade, the five-year-old son of Senator Morton J. Slade, is killed in Dodge City, someone's neck is bound to be stretched. Billie Flint makes a likely suspect — but when Born Gallant drifts into Dodge and sees the innocence on the accused's face, he reacts impulsively and snatches young Flint from certain death. Setting out to hunt down the real killer of the child, Gallant will soon learn that being the hero does not always mean doing what's right . . .

THE SILVER TRAIL

Ben Bridges

Carter O'Brien's gun is for hire, but only when the job — and the money — is right. As tough as they come, he's been everything from lawman to bounty hunter in his time. Right now he's riding shotgun on an expedition led by an old Army buddy. The goal: to find a lost canyon of silver down in Mexico. But the way is blocked not only by gunmen working for a greedy businessman, but also a ghost from O'Brien's past.

SNOWBOUND

Logan Winters

Private enquiry agent Carson Banner has been hired to track down Julian Prince's missing daughters — Candice, who has eloped with the no-good swindler Bill Saxon; and Ruth, who refused to let her younger sister go off alone with strangers. As a snowstorm out of Canada blows its way south across Dakota land, Banner must find the party before harm comes to the girls — or the blizzards kill them all . . .

RUTHLESS MEN

Corba Sunman

Provost Captain Slade Moran hunts down Private Daniel Green, a deserter from the 2nd Cavalry accused of murder. But, when arrested, Green swears he's innocent. Upon returning to the fort with his prisoner, Moran is informed that trouble has flared up in nearby Lodgepole, where a saloon gambler has been caught cheating and soldiers want revenge. Three men have already roughed up the cardsharp, and now the saloon has caught fire. All suspicion points towards the soldiers of Fort Collins . . .